A Stirring from Salem

A *Stirring* from Salem

Sheri Anderson

Based on characters from *Days of our Lives*,
originally created by Allan Chase, Ted Corday, and Irna Phillips

Days of our Lives
Publications

Published by Days of our Lives Publications, an imprint of Sourcebooks, Inc.
P.O. Box 4410, Naperville, Illinois 60567-4410
(630) 961-3900
Fax: (630) 961-2168
www.sourcebooks.com

Library of Congress Cataloging-in-Publication Data

Anderson, Sheri.
  Stirring from Salem / Sheri Anderson.
      p. cm.
  "Based on characters from Days of our Lives, originally created by Allan Chase, Ted Corday, and Irna Phillips."
  I. Days of our lives (Television program) II. Title.
PS3601.N5465S75 2011
813'.6—dc22
                                    2011004676

Printed and bound in the United States of America.
VP 10 9 8 7 6 5 4 3 2 1

Also by Sheri Anderson

A SECRET IN SALEM

For Phyllis and George,
whose son makes every day of my life a romance…

1  *CHARLEY*

FEW PLACES ON EARTH ARE AS DAZZLING AS LONDON ON New Year's Eve, and this year was no exception.

Hundreds of thousands of revelers swarmed the streets for miles around the Thames as they waited in the freezing night air for the most recognizable clock in the world, Big Ben, to strike midnight. The centuries-old celebration in historic Trafalgar Square had been relocated to the "London Eye," a massive Ferris wheel on the Thames that could be seen from all across the most visited city in the world. And when the ten-minute fireworks extravaganza started, London would erupt into glorious chaos.

Most people huddled together for warmth on the packed streets while they waited, but the glitterati were celebrating in the world-famous clubs and bars across London. Charley Gaines, a beautiful teenaged former heiress, and her brothers were at the hottest New Year's Eve party in the city at the rooftop club Rockwell.

Jubilation, passion, debauchery, and hope mingled in the air. Dom Pérignon corks popped. Everyone was there—from Princesses Beatrice and Eugenie to The Black Eyed Peas and Quentin Tarantino.

"Jackson," Charley said as she tapped her big brother on the shoulder, "I want to get out of here before the city goes mad."

There was no answer. Charley turned to see that he was in a lip-lock with Abby Deveraux. Jackson and Abby had been seeing each other off and on since they had met the previous summer in Monte Carlo. It had been a tumultuous summer for the Gaines family—a summer that had ended not only with the collapses of their father's financial empire and their mother's OMG fashion house, but with their parents' tragic deaths as well.

But this was New Year's Eve, and Jackson, Charley, and Chance were determined to put the old year's tragedies behind them as best they could. It's what their larger-than-life, full-of-pride, and totally image-conscious parents would have expected.

"It's not even midnight," Charley said, shaking her head with a smile. Then her other brother squeezed past her as he headed to his Tom-Ford-suited date. "Chance!" she shouted.

The next in line to the now-defunct Gaines throne was carrying two shots of Milagro Select. "Can I get you one, Sis?" Chance smiled, indicating the pricey liquor as he inched his way through the massive partying crowd. "It'll have to be after midnight."

"No, I'm leaving…and tequila's not my thing, in case you forgot!" she reminded him.

"But New Year's Eve is a time to celebrate. This last year is almost over," he said emphatically over the escalating din. "Only way to go is up."

"And we will!" Charley proclaimed a little too emphatically. "I feel it."

"Me, too," Chance lied. The Gaineses all hoped for the best but had learned to expect the worst.

Someone blew a paper horn in Charley's ear. It didn't matter that these were some of the wealthiest celebrities from around the globe; cheesy horns and noisemakers were at the ready.

"Ten..." the crowd started as the countdown all around Europe began.

"Oh, no!" Charley gasped.

"...nine..."

"See you tomorrow?" she yelled to her brother over the deafening noise.

"...eight..."

"Gotta go over our resolutions!" she continued, straining to be heard.

"...seven..."

"Bye!" She needed to make her getaway.

"SEX!"

Chance nodded, laughing cheekily at the crowd's countdown joke as he turned and handed his date the intoxicating drink.

"...five..."

"'Scuse me, 'scuse me!" Charley repeated as she shouldered her way through the crowd.

"...four...three..."

Time was running out, and Charley began to panic. If the club was a madhouse now, in ten minutes it would be a zoo. She was in a sea of Dolce & Gabbana, Prada, and even some cherished logos that represented her mother's internationally coveted OMG brand.

"Charley, how was your Christmas?" squeaky-voiced Dalita

Kasagian yelled, distracting Charley whose heel caught on the rug as she tried to avoid Dalita.

"…two…"

Charley lurched for the exit and struggled to keep from falling flat on her face. As she started to go down, the club went totally mad.

"Happy New Year!" Horns blared, people kissed, confetti flew, and fireworks filled the London sky. Charley fell into the arms of a tall, dark, and strikingly handsome man who was standing with a Eurotrash entourage behind him.

"Just who I was looking for." The man smiled evenly through pearly white teeth. "Charley Gaines."

Did he just say my name? she thought.

"Vincent Castle?" Charley gasped as she realized who he was.

Vince Castle was only the most successful photographer since Annie Leibovitz. Charley's mother had always wanted him for the OMG fashion layouts. And as an aspiring photographer herself, Charley was in total awe.

"Good eye." Vince smiled as he indicated the madness. "This is nuts."

Before she could agree, Vince wrapped his arm through hers and led her out of the party everyone in London would give their eyeteeth to be in.

As they made their way through dozens of kissing, groping, and dancing partyers, Charley was dumbstruck.

What does Vince Castle want from me?

2  *PATCH AND KAYLA*

As the clock hit twelve, the Eiffel Tower exploded with a profusion of fireworks that lit up the entire sky. It was the epitome of high romance on the Champs-Élysées as Parisians flooded the avenue.

"Happy New Year, Sweetness," the roughly handsome Steve "Patch" Johnson said to his wife as he tucked a spiky blonde lock of hair behind her ear.

"I love you, Steve," she replied with a look in her eye that let him know she meant it.

The countdown in the City of Lights was spectacular, especially viewed on the high-def TV in Steve and Kayla's magnificent chalet home in South Africa. He pulled her into a deep and very long kiss. It was as if they had set off the fireworks that were showering on the TV behind them.

Kayla responded fully. She did love this man, even if he was the antithesis of who everyone thought she'd marry.

They'd had a long and often rocky path to where they were now: happily married with a beautiful daughter living in the States and a scrappy two-year-old son, Joe, asleep in his room.

Steve, nicknamed Patch by those in their hometown Salem due to the eye patch he wore covering a decades-old injury, held his wife in his arms and twirled her as the party continued in the background. He pulled her back to him and danced close. Their bodies matched each movement as if they were one.

Sirens suddenly punctuated the festivities on the screen. The partying was turning into a full-out riot.

"Aren't you glad we're not there?" Steve laughed.

He pulled away from Kayla and went to turn off the electronic intrusion.

"Are you glad we're here?" Kayla asked sincerely.

"Why wouldn't I be?" Steve said as he took her hand and led her out onto the deck of their thatched home. "Look at this."

Kayla looked out into a clear summer night. South of the equator, the world was upside down, so New Year's Eve was during the heart of summer in their South African home. And Kayla loved it.

"Sometimes I wonder if this is just a dream," she admitted. "And I'm going to wake up back in Salem."

"It's not a dream, Sweetness," he said, smiling.

Steve took her hand and led her to a chaise lounge on the large wooden deck where they'd spent so many romantic moments. The moon shone brightly in the near-black sky. Millions of crystal-clear twinkling stars dotted the sky and could be seen all the way to the ground.

"Was the sky ever like this in Salem?" she asked.

"Nope, but don't tell 'em. We don't want a string of company," he said, smiling.

"We can always use more volunteers," she reminded him.

They were in the small town of Hoedspruit, just outside world-renowned Kruger National Park, for an extended stay. Kayla, a physician, oversaw the Tom-Ali Clinic, a small medical facility founded by Dr. Bill Horton to serve the magnificent game farms and also villagers who were in dire need of medical attention.

The clinic was named for Bill's parents, Tom and Alice, who had done so much for their hometown of Salem and the world that everyone seemed to want to honor them in some way.

Patch and Kayla lay for a moment drinking in the enveloping silence that was interrupted now and then by the sounds of South African nature, which included king crickets, exotic birds, and the rustling of leaves as the winds and wildlife moved through the bush.

"Lack of civilization," Steve murmured. "Who'd have thought I'd love it."

"You hear about the major photo shoot?" Kayla asked.

"That's now?" Steve asked.

She nodded. "This week. At one of the high-end game farms. One of the biggest photographers in the world is shooting it."

"Maybe one of his divas will wander off and get eaten." Steve grinned.

"No fat on their bones," Kayla answered.

"Skinny bitches," Steve scowled. "Blech."

"And another reason women adore you," she replied, smiling.

"How about I carry you back to our four-poster and have my way with you, woman." Steve grinned sexily.

"Thought you'd never ask."

They would have preferred to make love right there on the

deck under the blanket of stars or on the down sofa in the vaulted living room of the amazing thatched home that would be worth millions in the States. But they could lock the master suite with no fear of a surprise visit from their little son, Joe.

Steve placed Kayla on the bed and slipped the shoulder strap off her gauzy linen dress. Just then the phone rang.

"Happy New Year, whoever you are," Steve muttered.

"It could be Stephanie." Kayla gasped as he kissed her neck.

"A twenty-year-old calling her parents? I don't think so," he said, ignoring the ring. Candles on the side tables cast a soft glow on his wife. Her All-American face was more beautiful than ever.

The answering machine picked up. Steve kissed Kayla's bare shoulder.

"Kayla, it's Bill," a slurred voice said on the other side of the call.

The lovers felt as if a bucket of cold water had been splashed on them.

"A tracker was just brought to the clinic with a bullet hole in his shoulder and…"

Kayla picked up the phone.

"Bill?"

"Hey." Bill's voice was relieved but still shaky. "I left Cornelius a message to get over here but didn't hear back. I—have to leave," he stammered. "You're gonna need to handle it, Kayla. S-orry."

Kayla was startled to hear a dial tone. "Bill?" But he'd hung up.

"Something tells me we'd better get a move on," Steve said as he drank in what he'd heard.

Kayla was a mixture of disbelief and disappointment. "Bill was on call for emergencies tonight."

"And he knows he can count on you, come hell or high water," Steve answered. "We can take up where we left off later," he added, noticing her extreme frustration.

"As much as I'm disappointed we were interrupted, it's not that." Kayla offered. "I know it's New Year's Eve, but…he was on call, Steve," she repeated. "And I think he's drunk."

There was a long silence as Steve met her gaze.

"I've been meaning to talk to you about that," he admitted. "Lately, I think Bill's been hittin' the bottle."

3  *CHARLEY*

IT WAS NEARLY 8:00 A.M. WHEN CHARLEY HEARD THE KEY IN THE front door of the twelfth-floor Knightsbridge flat where she was living with Jackson.

While she adored both of her brothers equally, she preferred to stay with Jackson because Chance's flat in the trendy gay section of Soho had become known as Party Central. Besides, Jackson had three bedrooms in exclusive Kensington, not far from Holland Park, where they'd spent their childhoods in glorious surroundings. Once known for the literati, artists, and art collectors who had lived there in another century, the exclusive section was now home to the likes of Madonna and Simon Cowell.

As he entered the living room, which reeked of taste and money, Jackson was in an amazingly jolly mood for having been up all night.

"Oh, what a night, Sis!" He grinned as he pulled off the silk tie that was now loose around the neck of his Brunello Cucinelli cashmere tux.

"It was for us all," she said, smiling as she emerged from the hallway leading to her bedroom.

"You get lucky?" he joked, knowing his baby sister, who was a nineteen-year-old virgin, planned to remain as pure as the freshly driven snow. "I could use some hair of the dog," he added as he moved to the fully stocked bar in the corner of the living room.

"Actually, Jackson, I did get lucky," she said with a sultry tone. "*Really* lucky."

The protective older brother stopped in his tracks.

"Tell me you won the lottery," he said as he cocked his eyebrow questioningly.

"Better."

"What could be better than winning a double rollover? Remember last year?"

A group of six of their friends had indeed won last year's lotto to the tune of ten million euro. A win like that would have been spectacular, considering what the Gaineses had lost in a financial debacle that rivaled the Madoffs, but even those winnings would have only been a drop in the family bucket.

Yes, they were lucky enough to have a benefactor who had paid off a portion of the multimillions involved. But new victims were still coming out of the woodwork, claiming that the Gaines children were responsible for their losses. The pressure of taking responsibility for his father's sins had driven Bernie Madoff's son to commit suicide. The Gaines siblings were determined not to let that be their future.

"Money is just money," Charley said coolly. "And yes, that would help you hang on to your flat and pay for me to go to an art institute for my photography…"

"And?"

"Are you blind?" she answered, turning him to face a suitcase and carry-on open on the living-room sofa. "Ta-da."

"I assume you're going somewhere?"

"Guess," she insisted.

"Switzerland?" he asked carefully. Switzerland was his first choice because John and Marlena Evans Black, two of the most amazing people on the planet, lived in Lausanne. And when the financial debacle had happened the previous summer, part of the massive fallout had been the revelation that they, not Richie and Olivia Gaines, were Charley's biological parents.

"No…"

"Dalita Kasagian did not invite you to Anguilla, did she?"

"No…" Charley scowled. "And hanging with her crowd would be the *unluckiest* thing that could happen." Dalita, God bless her, was known for being the daughter of one of the wealthiest men in the world and had always been kelly-green jealous of naturally gorgeous Charley. But since the tragic accident that had taken Olivia's life the summer before, Dalita had wanted nothing more than to be seen as sympathetic to "poor Charley."

Dalita was constantly telling her sycophants that she felt guilty since Charley and Olivia had been on their way to her grossly ostentatious Sweet Sixteen bash when their car had careened off the Grande Corniche above Monte Carlo. Truth be told, Dalita had not felt guilty when it happened, but she had been upset that news of the accident had stolen the thunder from her celebrity-studded party.

"If not with Dalita, maybe New York," Jackson guessed next.

"No."

"Cabo?"

"No!"

"Singapore, Rio, Amsterdam—"

"No, no, no. I'm going to South Africa!"

"Really?" he said startled.

"Absolutely."

"When?"

"Tonight."

"How?" he stammered. To travel anywhere at the last minute was more difficult than winning that lottery.

"One of the most amazing photographers in the world is shooting the cover of *The Look*'s twentieth anniversary issue, and his assistant came down with pneumonia. He's hiring me to take her place. We're taking British Airways, and we leave tonight at seven."

She didn't see Jackson blanch.

"Is it Vince Castle?" he asked carefully.

"Yes! Isn't that fantastic?" Charley was elated.

Jackson studied her luminous face. In the last year, it had had more frowns than smiles, and he was happy to see the change. Whatever issues he had with the photographer were trumped by her excitement. "You know, Sis, it really is fantastic. Congratulations."

"Having a new start was one of my resolutions for this year, Jackson," she said, smiling warmly. "And it's already coming true."

"I resolved to be less impulsive," Jackson admitted.

"With women especially," Charley cautioned.

"Amen," Jackson agreed.

The handsome, charismatic heir to a fortune had been a chick magnet since he was old enough to understand the appeal of the floppy hair that skimmed his eyebrows.

"You never understood that leading a woman on is worse than rejecting her," Charley added.

With that, Jackson's chiseled face fell as a wave of the details of the previous night washed over him. "Uh-oh."

"What?" Charley knew that expression.

Jackson reached inside his Brioni shirt and felt the empty chain around his neck.

"Mum's...ring," he stammered.

"Not again!" Charley groaned.

Jackson nodded. "Yep. I think I just asked another woman to marry me."

4   *ABBY*

ROMANCE HAD ALWAYS BEEN TOUGH FOR ABBY DEVERAUX.

Her mother, Jennifer Deveraux, had never been without a man lusting after her. Jennifer, blonde and absolutely adorable from her first day in kindergarten, had never realized the effect she had on the opposite sex as she grew older.

Abby's father, Jack, with his captivating mix of sophistication and silliness, was Jennifer's perfect match. An adoring father, he doted on Abby who was a natural blonde like her mother, grandmother Laura, and great-grandmother Alice Horton. Especially since he'd been an absentee father during a lot of Abby's formative years.

Abby was actually beautiful, too, though she never truly felt it. Gawky and awkward through her early teens, she was always in the shadow of her cheerleader-pretty mother.

Abby shared an apartment in London's Primrose Hill, which in recent years had become one of the hubs for those in the media and entertainment business. Local residents included Gwyneth Paltrow, Gwen Stefani, and Ewan McGregor.

Her iPhone rang, startling her out of a deep, near-catatonic sleep. As the celebrated editor of Spectator.com, one of the hottest news and gossip sites worldwide, Abby was used to getting calls and hot tips at any time of the day from her stringers. That was something she had loved when she was starting the site, but sometimes the timing was lousy. Her cell was on the skirted table next to her bed, and she groped to answer it.

"You got me," Abby groaned as she cleared her throat.

"Happy New Year!"

It was her father.

"What…time is it?" Abby asked as she struggled to sit on the edge of her queen-sized bed and tried to orient herself.

"Just after midnight in Salem," Jack offered.

"Are you with Mom?" Abby asked. Her parents had separated once more, but she was hopeful.

"She has her own life now, you know, but I'm going to try to see her," he answered. Though trying to sound confident, his voice cracked as he changed the subject. "You've done a great job this year, baby. I just wanted you to know how much your mother and I love you."

"Thanks, Daddy," Abby said, managing a smile. "I love you, too."

She did love them both and missed them. Her mother had gone back to the Midwest for a while to help one of her cousins, and the off-again, on-again love of Jennifer's life had gone to Australia on "walkabout," one of his unpredictable sojourns.

"And don't worry, I know everything's good at the paper."

The Spectator, the newspaper for which Jack was publisher, had finally gotten back on its feet and was running like a top, even with the struggling economy. That was largely due to Abby's success with its new media component, which she had started as a sideline while she was finishing her education.

"Go back to sleep," Jack said. "I hope your New Year's Eve was wonderful."

The fog began to clear in Abby's alcohol-saturated brain.

She took the phone from her ear and looked at her left hand. There it was: a four-carat yellow diamond.

"Abby...?" her dad said. "Honey, you still there?"

"I...am..." she stammered. "And, well, Dad—I got engaged!" she shouted excitedly.

"You got what?"

"'Engaged!' as in asked to get married!" Abby blubbered.

"Not to that playboy, unable-to-find-a-job-because-of-his-family's-reputation Jackson Gaines, right?"

"Of course not, Daddy," Abby said in the voice that always melted Jack's heart. "The fabulous, funny, sexy as hell, and destined to greatness Jackson Gaines. Be happy for me."

"You cannot marry that man, Abigail Deveraux," Jack insisted.

"Is that an order?" Abby said as her back went up.

"Yes!"

"I love you, Daddy," Abby said, ignoring his demand. "And Happy New Year."

With that, she hung up and sighed heavily.

He is a good man, Daddy, Abby thought as she gazed at the gorgeous diamond. Not like his father at all. A good man who I am going to marry!

As the realization washed over her, she broke into a huge, overwhelmed smile. "Yes, yes, yes!" Abby squealed and began to jump around the room excitedly. Just then her best friend and flatmate, Chelsea Brady, stopped into the open doorway.

"What the heck's going on, Abs?" Chelsea asked as she fought back emotions of her own.

"Look!" Abby dashed to her best friend and thrust the exquisite ring in front of her. "Jackson asked me to marry him last night," Abby beamed.

Chelsea's big brown eyes widened as the reality hit her. "That's great," she said with a weak smile.

"And you?" Abby asked excitedly. "I know Max had something major to talk about…"

Max and Chelsea had dated off and on for four years, and he was the love of her life. Chelsea bit her lip.

"Well?" Abby asked, her eyes narrowing.

"Let's just say he did not propose!" Chelsea blurted.

"Wow," Abby blanched.

"Yeah, wow," Chelsea snapped and then burst into a sea of tears.

5  *MARLENA AND JOHN*

MAISON DU NOIR—THE HOUSE OF BLACK—WAS EVEN more spectacular in winter than in summer. The villa was perfectly situated in Lausanne with the soaring white-peaked Swiss Alps on one side and Lake Geneva in front. It was picture-postcard perfect.

Though the ground was covered with a dusting of white, Marlena Evans took her morning walk through the fields in front of the contemporary glass, wood, and steel structure. The home, designed by the one of the top architects in Europe and supervised by John, was often the talk of the locals.

Marlena wrapped her arms around herself to steel herself from the cold.

"Doc?" she heard from behind, and she turned to see the man she cherished trotting toward her from their first-floor gym. John's six-foot frame was shirtless, and he wore only workout shorts and sneakers. Behind him, through the floor-to-ceiling windows, she could see the workout space he'd installed with every imaginable piece of equipment to keep up his rehabilitation. It was a place where John spent a great deal of time, even on New Year's Day.

"You're going to catch your death of cold, mister," she scolded.

"It helps me be strong like bull," he said with a fake Russian accent, smiling and flexing his well-toned biceps.

"That sounds like bull," she said, shivering, and added, "Is that how the ISA trained you?" The ISA—the International Security Alliance—an organization John had once worked for in one of his many incarnations, was known for its grueling physical requirements.

"Nope, this is my own doing," John admitted. "And you're right, it is cold out here!"

He wrapped his arm around her slim shoulders and they headed back to the house.

"What time is that parade you wanted to watch?" he said.

Distracted, Marlena didn't answer.

"You're not *really* mad at me, are you?" he asked.

"About what?" she asked.

"Our discussion last night? My suggestion we go helicopter skiing?"

With their plans in flux, John had suggested a number of ways to spend the rest of the holiday. The adrenaline-pumping sport of helicopter skiing was one of them.

"Actually, I'd forgotten about that so of course I wasn't *mad* about it," she interrupted. "But now that you bring it up again, while I know it's supposed to be safe, the idea of you jumping out of a helicopter at four thousand feet makes my blood run cold."

"It's the snow that does that," he tried joking.

She stopped in her tracks and took a deep breath. Maybe this was a better discussion than the one she wanted. "I've lost you too many times, and it scares the living heck out of me."

"Heck," he mocked her lightly to deflect the seriousness. "You're the one who was born skiing in Colorado, Doc."

"I know," she responded. "And loving snow is in my genes. But—"

"We've got nothing in our future but time," he reminded her. "Can we at least think about it?"

John knew he didn't need Marlena's permission to do anything. He never had, and she would never want him to. But he also knew that, as a loving husband, he needed to be sensitive to her and to any fears she had about him being in dangerous situations.

"We'll think about it," she said, smiling wanly. "Now let's get inside. You're freezing! And that parade is at noon London time."

The parade she wanted to see was the London New Year's Day parade, which had become her favorite. A small-town girl at heart, she had grown up watching the Rose Parade every year, and this was a damned good substitution. No magnificent flower-covered floats but the same exuberance with London as its backdrop and participants from every corner of the world.

What could be better?

∞

They entered the exquisite villa that had been their home for the last few years. They had moved to Switzerland for the most comprehensive medical care John could get after he'd been paralyzed from the neck down at the hands of a lunatic. By the time he'd recovered, they had fallen in love with the location and decided to stay.

The cut-glass door closed behind them, and the warmth of the home enveloped them.

"Better," he admitted. "Smells good in here."

"Oven pancake." She smiled. Marlena had never been a great cook, but she had mastered some simple holiday staples. "Then the pre-parade show?" she asked.

"Sure," John agreed, smiling. He knew Marlena loved her family traditions, and he was ready to share them even though they drove him a bit crazy. For the last few years, she'd devoted herself totally to him, so it was the least he could do. "Lemme get showered."

"Please do," she managed to respond, smiling back at him.

"I love you, Doc," he reminded her and kissed the tip of her nose. "And that face…"

Her eyes met his. He cocked his eyebrow, as he'd been known to do on more than one occasion, and smiled the smile she found irresistible.

"And I adore you," she answered.

John leaned in to give her a deep kiss that reminded her why and then bounded up the staircase to the massive suite he had designed just for her.

She watched him go and for a moment focused on the magnificent eagle tattoo on his back. The elegant bird of prey had been inked over a phoenix tattoo that had marked John as the pawn of his nemesis, Stefano DiMera. Now it was a symbol of the man he'd become again in the last six months.

After shrugging out of her jacket, Marlena moved to the ceiling-high Scots Pine with thousands of lights that had stood in front of the window since a week before Christmas.

Marlena sighed and moved to take in the entire vista. The city, with its charm and warmth and history, was coming alive. As for Marlena? She wasn't.

Life is supposed to be perfect now, she thought. Then why am I starting to feel so empty?

∞

John Black's life had been an enigma since he was born. He was a beautiful child who had turned into a more beautiful man, but his tumultuous path had made him the man he was today: a man of integrity, a man of strength, and a brilliant mind behind a movie star–handsome face.

A man so in love with Marlena Evans that he did not want to lose her and would never do anything to risk that. But still, thoughts lingered…

Steaming water in their hundred-thousand-dollar bathroom streamed over John's body, warming him from his chilly jaunt outside. After he'd finished buffing his skin with the finest men's products, he stepped out of the shower to the marble sink to shave. As he turned on the water, John noticed the tip of the eagle's wing on the top of his shoulder.

Not a phoenix to rise but an eagle to soar, he thought to himself. Then why am I feeling grounded?

6  *TOM-ALI CLINIC*

BILL HORTON HAD OPENED THE TOM-ALI CLINIC IN THE mid-'90s after he'd gone on a trip with Doctors Without Borders and fallen in love with Africa. The incredible beauty and serenity to be found in the Limpopo province was only matched by the desperate need that he could help fill.

Positioned on the outskirts of the small hub city of Hoedspruit, the privately funded clinic had helped thousands and thousands over the years. Though now in need of repair, it had a reception area, two exam rooms, a small emergency room, and storage, plus a barbed-wire-walled outdoor space where patients would line up for the free medical services offered by volunteers who came from around the world.

An armed guard was at the locked building twenty-four hours a day to discourage theft and squatters. Tom-Ali had also added a fully equipped mobile van several years earlier to go into the African villages that still dotted the outskirts of the mainly Afrikaner towns and cities.

Recently, Kayla had committed to being at Tom-Ali for two

years, with occasional trips back to the States as time permitted and others filled in for her. And of all the doctors who'd been there, Kayla Brady was far and away the favorite of the locals.

Compassionate, caring, and gentle, and with skills comparable to those of the top general practitioners in South Africa, Kayla treated black and white, male and female, young and old with the same level of care and the same smile she gave her own children.

Steve was loved in a different way. While Kayla was the healer, Steve was the clinic's protector. A jack-of-all-trades, he was the master of many. In an area sometimes gripped with fear, he had none. He was the ideal balance for Kayla. While Steve was quick to anger, Kayla was the epitome of cool.

Except today. Today she was furious. Bill Horton was nowhere to be found.

The last she'd heard from Bill had been the call well after midnight. To top it off, when she and Steve had arrived at the clinic in the dead of night, the mobile van was missing. The security officer's wound had been much more severe than Bill had told her. She had staunched the flow of blood and pumped the man full of fluids and morphine while Steve alerted emergency personnel to medevac the dying twenty-five-year-old on an hour-long flight to Johannesburg General Hospital. Now the sun was up and she was exhausted.

"Have you heard anything, Sweetness?" Steve asked as he entered from one of the storerooms.

"From Bill?" she asked.

"Jo'burg General."

"That poor boy lost nearly three pints of blood before he got there, but by the grace of God, he's still alive."

"The grace of Dr. Kayla Brady," Steve corrected her. "Without you, he'd have died on the way."

"Bill left him here with the tracker!" she bellowed.

"There has to be an explanation," Steve said, trying to calm her.

The rear door to the clinic clicked open and Cornelius entered. In his mid-twenties, the Cape Town–born volunteer was normally the most reliable worker they had. He'd taken a year off from getting his veterinary degree to devote his time to the clinic.

"Where the hell were you?" Kayla demanded, startling both Steve and their assistant. Kayla Brady did not use four-letter words. Ever.

"A fight broke out last night over at Malivana," Cornelius answered. Malivana was a small game farm an hour the other side of Hoedspruit. "I took the call and didn't want to disturb the two of you. I thought you deserved a quiet New Year's Eve."

"Well, we didn't have one," Kayla answered. She took a few deep breaths. "What did you find over there?"

"I never made it, but I hear it was a tempest in a teapot—or more of a whisky bottle," Cornelius admitted.

"Why didn't you get there?" Kayla wondered.

"The van blew a tire halfway there."

"There was no spare?" Steve asked.

"Nope. I spent the night in the van. Sometimes one forgets how bright the night sky is in Africa—and how few mechanics are open on New Year's Day. Especially in Hoedspruit."

Kayla sighed. "I'm truly sorry, Cornelius. But why no spare?"

"Ask Dr. Horton," he answered simply.

The moment was broken as Kayla's cell phone rang. She answered abruptly. "Dr. Brady."

"Kayla, it's Marlena. We wanted to wish you and Patch a Happy New Year. Is this a bad time?"

Kayla realized her agitation was clear as a bell to Marlena. The two had become especially close during their last few months in Salem and read each other well.

"I just need to get in touch with Bill, and…" Kayla stopped and took a deep calming breath. "Please, give our love to John. I hear he's fully recovered and all's well there."

"It's wonderful," Marlena said. *At least it should be.*

Just then, another call came through on Kayla's cell. The caller ID said B HORTON. "It's Bill, Marlena, can I call you back?"

"Any time," Marlena said. "Tell him we miss him, too."

Kayla pushed the "flash" button on her phone. "Bill?"

But there was no answer. She tried a redial to the number, which was his landline at home. His voicemail answered.

Kayla was more frustrated than ever.

"Sweetness, you should get back to Joe," Steve reminded Kayla calmly. "Let me drop you off and go to Bill's to see what's up."

Kayla knew he was right. Though it was still morning, Kayla was indeed fading. And she knew their Xhosa housekeeper, Violet, had been promised New Year's Day off to spend with her husband and son. Besides, if Kayla saw Bill now, she might throttle him.

"I'll stock the van for tomorrow," Cornelius offered. "I know you wanted to get over to the Mapusha weavers tomorrow."

"Thank you both," Kayla agreed. Then she added wryly, "Happy New Year."

Steve escorted his exhausted wife out to their Jeep, which was parked next to the van at the rear of the clinic. The Rover was stifling from the searing summer sun, so Steve immediately turned on the air conditioning full blast.

Cornelius waited in the open doorway until the Jeep disappeared down the gravel highway and into the lush foliage. He then signaled the guard, who slung his rifle over his shoulder and joined Cornelius at the rear of the van.

Inside the Tom-Ali van were two large cardboard boxes. The guard quickly hoisted them, one on top of the other, and then carried them into the clinic. Cornelius nonchalantly made sure they had not been observed and then bolted the back door of the clinic behind them.

7  *CHARLEY*

I<small>F THE STREETS OF</small> L<small>ONDON WERE A MADHOUSE ON</small> N<small>EW</small> Year's Eve, they were even worse the next morning. The New Year's Parade was expected to be bigger than ever for its twenty-fifth anniversary, with more than ten thousand performers participating from around the world. Dance troops, marching bands, clowns, and acrobats. More than a half million people would crowd the two-mile route from Parliament Square to Piccadilly. Some of them had camped over and were suffering from the night before, while others were arriving in droves to view the spectacle.

In other words, with the parade starting when Big Ben struck noon, if you had someplace to get to, one of the worst times of the year to be in the center of London was 11:00 a.m. on New Year's Day.

But Charley had to get ready to leave for Africa that night so she needed lightweight khakis and malaria tablets. Where better to find them on short notice in London than Harrods?

"Thank you, thank you, thank you," she said to Chance as they hurried out of Kingston House South and into the bitter cold.

"Happy to help," Chance offered as they crossed through the serenely beautiful Ennismore neighborhood. "But why did Jackson have to bail?"

"He had to go see his fiancée," Charley answered. She was walking at a fast clip. "You up to walking?"

"Not again," Chance groaned.

"It's less than ten minutes," she said, misunderstanding.

"I meant about Jackson. Abby Deveraux?" he questioned. Jackson and Abby had only been dating for a few months, but Chance knew his impulsive brother well.

"He's going to see her now," Charley responded with a look Chance knew well. "Come on, so much to do!"

The brother and sister crossed over to Brompton Road and made their way to the most famous department store in the world, Harrods of London.

∞

Once known for the royal warrants awarded for serving the Queen for nearly two hundred years, Harrods was now more like an amusement park for shoppers. The massive store had more than three hundred departments and was a zoo for more reasons than one. Not only was it one of the largest department stores in the world, but it also had massive sales starting on New Year's Day. The times had changed from when holidays were family time—now they honored the heights of consumerism.

From top to tail, the store was still replete with thousands of Christmas decorations, starting with more than twelve thousand lights that ringed the store's block-long exterior. Inside were hundreds of lavish Christmas trees and gaily wrapped packages, as well as elves, faeries, and gnomes. Angels with silver-tipped wings and snowmen as big and cold as refrigerators. Reindeer and bright red sleighs. Christmas carols piped in throughout the store. At least for a few more days.

It had been a family tradition for her mother, Olivia, to take Charley to see Father Christmas at Harrods' second-floor grotto every year as a child, starting when she was two. Decked out in fur with her perfectly coiffed hair and movie-star makeup, Olivia had offered flirtatious winks whenever she saw the jolly fat man in the red suit and had created incredible moments for Charley to remember.

Once Charley was too old for those visits, she and her mother had still made nostalgic annual trips to Harrods. But this year, just six months after her mother's death, Charley hadn't stepped inside the store during the holiday season.

When she and Chance walked through the front entrance, it all struck her.

"I'll hit the chemist first," Chance said, picking up a brisk pace. "You're headed to malaria country...you need to take the tablets right away. You hear me?"

There was no answer. Chance realized he was walking alone.

Ten feet behind him, standing stock-still in the center of the bustling aisle, was Charley. All around her she could see the international women's designer labels.

"Sis?" he said, approaching her. "You okay?"

"Sure," she said quietly.

Chance realized they were surrounded by the fashions that had once been competitors of their mother's now-in-limbo label.

"Sorry," he sighed.

"I am so lucky I have you and Jackson," Charley said, choking back unexpected tears. "But I miss Mummy and even Dad," she admitted for the first time in months. "Whatever unspeakable things he did, he was our father."

8  *ABBY*

"I'm happy for you, Abby. I really am," Chelsea said, sniffling.

"If only my dad was," Abby admitted.

The exquisitely cut diamond on her finger seemed to catch fire as it was hit directly by a ray of light shining through the large bay window that looked out on Regent's Park.

"With my parents' crazy history, I don't know how Dad could judge me. With my luck, Mom will, too."

Throughout Abby's childhood and into her teens, Jack and Jennifer had gone through a divorce, abandonment, and life-threatening illness before they made their way back to each other. Their love for their daughter had never wavered, but the uncertainty and miscommunication in her parents' relationship had made Abby cautious about love.

Until she met Jackson.

As the son of one of the most influential and social couples in the international jet set, Jackson had a je ne sais quoi unlike any of the boys she'd dated in Salem.

"They're your parents," Chelsea sighed with a hint of envy. "They're supposed to judge you. It means they care."

Chelsea's own background as an adopted and then orphaned child was more difficult than Abby's, and resentment had sent her into a tailspin as a teenager. She had once been a horrific influence on the willing Abby, but they'd both grown up and were now as close as two friends could be.

"Your parents care for you, too. I know you heard from your dad over the holidays, and even Hope..." Abby said. "Your mom definitely adores you. I would have loved to have had Billie Reed as my mom." Abby smiled and then tried her best to change the subject. "And hey, we have a wedding to plan!"

In fact, that made everything worse. "These tears aren't about my parents," Chelsea said. "Max dumped me last night."

Max had been her off-and-on boyfriend for more than four years. Whatever they'd been through, Chelsea had always believed that they'd be together forever.

Abby's heart sank for her friend. "I'm so, so sorry..."

The intercom buzzed.

Abby pushed the button, confused. She wasn't expecting anyone. "Yes?"

"It's me."

"Jackson?" she said, startled.

"Didn't you get my text?" he asked, having heard the tone in her voice.

"My phone's in the bedroom," she answered. "Chels and I've been having a chat, but come in, come in." She released the intercom button. "Sorry again," she said, grimacing at Chelsea.

"Don't be silly," Chelsea said, managing a smile.

A light triple tap said Jackson had gotten there within seconds.

Abby finger-combed her still tousled mane as she opened the door to her future husband.

"Hey, I'm a mess, I know. Sorry," she said coyly.

The moment was awkward. While she hadn't showered or changed, Jackson was his usual immaculate self. He was casually handsome in a brown leather duster that matched his dark hair and jeans that were worn in just the right places.

"You're beautiful," Jackson said. With the glow in her eyes, she truly was.

"I'm really happy for you, Jackson," Chelsea said as she took a deep breath.

"Right," was all he could say. "Abby, why don't we grab a bite over at The Engineer?"

The Engineer was Abby's favorite spot for breakfast, and it was open even on New Year's Day.

"Sure! Let me jump in the shower." Abby smiled. "I love you."

"You, too." Jackson gave her a half smile back.

Abby put her arms around him and kissed his neck sweetly, whispering, "Max broke up with Chelsea last night." Then she scampered off to get ready.

"I heard that," Chelsea admitted.

"He can be a bit of a jerk," Jackson offered.

"Not really," Chelsea said. "But thanks for trying to make me feel better."

Jackson nodded, and Chelsea finally smiled. "You know, I've never seen Abby so happy. And this news gives me faith that love still exists. Thanks for that, too."

She didn't notice Jackson shift uncomfortably.

"Her dad wasn't exactly thrilled with the news, but—"

"She already told her father?" Jackson asked.

"Yep, and she told him to stuff it!" Chelsea was actually laughing. "You know, I really did need this. There really is true love in the world!"

Great, Jackson thought. Getting the ring back is not going to be easy.

9  *SCARLETT*

SCARLETT WAS DOOMED TO A LIFE OF DRAMA FROM THE moment her mother saw her full head of bright red hair. The fact that their last name was O'Hara sealed the deal.

Originally from Atlanta, Scarlett was in New York at the age of fourteen for the Modeling Association of America International competition when she was discovered while peering into the windows of Tiffany & Co.

That had been in 1985—the year the first dot-com was registered. When Nelson Mandela was still incarcerated on Robbens Island. When Michael Jackson and Lionel Richie gathered their friends to perform "We Are the World" and the Live Aid concerts took place, all raising millions for the starving in Africa. Back then, Africa had seemed such a distant place…

Now, so many years later, she was going there.

"Shit," she said as she looked at her reflection in the beveled mirror in her suite at the London Hilton on Park Lane.

Scarlett's porcelain skin had always been one of her most valuable assets, but it was showing signs of her thirty-nine years. The face she saw in the mirror was not the one she'd seen on the dozens of magazine covers, from *Cosmopolitan* to *Vogue*, that she'd graced in more than twenty-five years on the modeling scene. Sure, Photoshop could erase the crow's feet and fine lines around her pouty lips. But for a woman once deemed "The Look," that wasn't much consolation.

At least Vince Castle was the photographer for this shoot. Scarlett had been his muse since the cover he'd shot of her for *The Look* had resulted in the magazine skyrocketing to its first sales of more than one million copies. Now they would be shooting the twentieth anniversary edition of that issue, and she was bloody nervous.

When her agent had told her she'd be sharing the cover and editorial with a new Swedish blonde, eighteen-year-old Brigitta, and stunning, twenty-seven-year-old, milk-chocolate-skinned Nikki Kovacs, Scarlett had thrown one of the screaming fits she'd become famous for. Now she wished she hadn't. Mimicking the extreme facial expressions from her tirades over the decades, she realized what a toll those expressions had taken.

"And shit!" she repeated.

The phone rang. She jumped, startled, and then answered. "Yes."

"Miss O'Hara, your facial and massage were at eleven," the clipped British voice said. It was Purity Mind & Body, the spa located in the hotel.

"Yes?" she repeated.

"It's 12:30. We have other guests scheduled at three."

"And so?" Scarlett answered with incredulity.

"Shall we cancel you?"

"I'll be five minutes! Do you have any idea who—"

"We'll see you then, ma'am," the voice interrupted.

Scarlett blanched as she heard a click.

"Ma'am? Shit," she muttered under her breath. The entire point of this shoot was to give her a chance for resurgence. She needed to be as relaxed and pampered as possible.

Wearing nothing but her hotel robe over her still-toned size two frame, she moved into the living room and opened the mini-bar. Two small bottles of vodka went into her robe pocket, and she dumped a third into a glass of orange juice.

She looked around her room. The Park Lane Hilton wasn't the most exclusive hotel in the city. But adjoining it was Whisky Mist, currently the hang for the likes of George Clooney, Jennifer Aniston, Kate Moss, Chloe Green, and the royals. Scarlett liked being in that crowd. She always had.

Glancing out across Hyde Park, she could see stragglers heading toward the end of the parade route.

"You know who I am? Don't you?" she said quietly. Then she downed the stiff libation.

10  *BILL*

BILL WAS NURSING AN UNBELIEVABLE HANGOVER WHEN HE heard Patch's Jeep pull into the gravel driveway.

He was not ready for company, especially Patch.

The year had been a long one for Bill Horton. Both his older brother, Mickey, and his beloved mother, Alice, had died. The year anniversary of Mickey's death was in a week, and it weighed heavily on Bill's shoulders. Had he been in Salem at the time, would he have been able to save his brother?

The answer, of course, was no. Mickey had died of a massive heart attack before the paramedics arrived, so even the most celebrated heart surgeon in the world would have been helpless.

The brothers had had a long and complicated relationship. They had been in love with the same woman, Laura, who had borne a child who was Bill's biological son but who had grown up thinking Mickey was his father.

Laura was now Bill's estranged wife, and he'd seen her again at his mother's funeral. He'd also seen his daughter, Jennifer, and his son, Lucas, who was the product of an illicit relationship years earlier. All in all, it had been an emotionally tumultuous time.

The doorbell rang.

Bill sighed and then got up from his leather chair. Over the hills, a crack of lightning lit up the sky, signaling an encroaching thunderstorm.

"Hey," Bill said as he opened the door.

"Hey," Patch answered. "Can I come in?"

"If I said no, would it make a difference?" Bill asked lightly. He and Patch had become friends. He didn't dislike the guy, but he wasn't in the mood for company.

"Not really," Patch said, entering.

"Some iced tea?" Bill offered.

"Sure."

Bill padded to the kitchen and took a pitcher of sweet tea from the fridge. Nothing was said as Bill poured a tall glass for Patch. Nothing had to be said.

Patch took a long drink. "He lost a lot of blood, but he made it."

"Great." Bill sighed with relief. "From what I could tell, he was shot by some bastard trying to poach a rhino."

"I hear the guy succeeded."

"Too many of them do," Bill said.

The desire for rhino horn had escalated tremendously since they'd opened the clinic. More than two hundred rhino had been poached in South Africa alone in the past year. While rhino horn had always been cherished by wealthy Chinese for use in herbal medicines and for aphrodisiacs, it had recently gained more popularity than ever around the world, even though science had proven it produced nothing more than a placebo effect.

"At eight thousand for an ounce of powdered horn on the black market, I guess that'll happen," Patch admitted.

There was a long silence, punctuated by one of the quick summer downpours that could happen on a moment's notice.

"Wish I could tell you what happened, Patch, but I'm clueless."

"You left Kayla holding the bag. Or the scalpel, I guess."

"And the last thing I remember is driving into Ngala." Bill noticed Patch's quizzical expression. "I had a quick one with Cornelius at the Trading Post and then headed for New Year's Eve drinks with the VP from First National in Jo'burg. I got the call about the ranger on my way and called Cornelius, then you."

"He never got the message," Patch said.

"I called him," Bill said, defending himself. "Then Kayla."

"What was so important at Ngala?" Patch queried.

"Mueller, the VP," Bill said. "I heard that guy never stops working, even on a holiday. At least I hoped so."

Bill's expression was glum. The lines on his handsome but well-worn face were more prominent than ever.

"Talk to me."

"I am so sorry." Bill sighed heavily. "We're broke, Patch. We'll be flat broke at the end of this month. He's my last gasp."

"We? You mean Tom-Ali?"

Bill nodded. "Ever hear of a guy named Richard Gaines?"

"Don't think so."

"Like Bernie Madoff, but his scheme seemed to mostly attract those of us in the health industry. I met him at a medical convention in Paris five years ago and sank every cent we had into his hedge fund. One of those too-good-to-be-trues. And it was."

"A lot of people depend on this clinic," Patch reminded him.

"To have the place named after my folks go under will kill me," Bill offered. "Mueller put me off until next week, but that may be too damned late. Please, don't tell Kayla until after that last meeting. I beg you. Do not let anyone know."

"Bill…"

"Promise me." Bill was adamant.

"Promise. But is that why you've been in your cups so much lately, Bud?" Patch asked while looking him squarely in the eye.

"Strange thing is, I haven't been overindulging," Bill answered.

"The slurred speech, the forgetting things?" Patch added. "Really out of character for you, man."

"Oh, I know it's been happening," Bill admitted, concerned about it himself. "I just don't know why."

11 KAYLA, JOHN, AND MARLENA

"Mommy!" Joe squealed. He flew to Kayla as she walked in the door.

Seeing Joe always put a smile on Kayla's face. Well, almost always. When she was exhausted, as she was this morning, she wished Steve was with her to absorb Joe's energy.

"Play with me!" Joe said as he grabbed her hand.

"I will, sweet boy," she agreed. "Just give me a few minutes with Violet."

Violet appeared from the kitchen, wiping her hands.

"We made mud pies, Mrs. Kayla." Violet smiled.

"Want some, Mommy?" Joe asked. "Where's Pop?"

"Taking care of some things," she answered simply. "He'll be home soon."

"Can we play? Let's play soldier!" Joe said, taking a stance as if holding a gun. "Bang!"

Kayla blanched. "How about playing mechanic instead?" she asked. No matter that they were in Africa and had several guns in the house, Kayla was not a fan of war games.

"Bang!" Joe repeated. "You're dead!"

Kayla gave him an admonishing look. He turned the pretend gun on Violet. "Bang!"

Violet pretended to fall back, and Joe giggled happily. "Let's build a fort!" he said, tossing the imaginary gun to the floor. "Come on, Mommy."

He tugged at her pant leg.

"Let's let your mommy rest a few minutes, my big little man." Violet smiled. Her warm and wide smile crinkled the corners of her deep brown eyes and always made Kayla feel better. "Just ten minutes," Violet added with a directive to Joe that let him know she meant business.

Joe nodded and shuffled off with Violet. "Darn it," he grumbled under his breath, which made Kayla smile. Her son was a rambunctious one, but for being just over two years old, he was both articulate and compliant.

Kayla put her satchel on the African mahogany dining table and took out her phone to charge it. She thought about how in Africa, the phone had become as important a doctor's tool as her stethoscope and syringes.

As she was about to plug it in, she remembered her terse conversation with Marlena. She checked the time and selected Marlena's cell number.

After two rings, Marlena answered. "Kayla, hi. You didn't need to call back."

"I just didn't want to leave you hanging," Kayla answered. "Is this a bad time?"

"No, of course not," Marlena said. Actually she was wrapped

in John's arms on their living-room sofa, watching the end of the parade, but she didn't want to lose the chance to talk to Kayla. "I always love hearing a voice from home."

As she sat up to talk, John noticed Marlena's demeanor change. She seemed more relaxed than she had been over the holidays.

"Didn't want you left hanging about Bill. I know you were close," Kayla said gently.

"What's going on?" Marlena asked.

"We don't know, but he's been acting strangely lately," Kayla admitted. "I hadn't said anything to Steve before, hoping I was imagining it, but now I'm worried. Bill always seems distracted and then forgets things. He's just not himself."

"Should I call him?" Marlena asked.

John could hear the tone in her voice.

"Steve's over talking to him now," Kayla answered. "Why don't I let you know what he finds out, if anything?"

"Probably the best idea," Marlena admitted. "I'll wait to hear from you."

"Once again, Happy New Year. And I love hearing a voice from home, too. It was nice talking with you," Kayla said.

"You, too. Bye-bye," Marlena said. She hung up the phone and held it in her hand for a long moment. Then she turned to John to explain. "Apparently, Bill Horton's been acting out of character."

"I got that," John said.

Marlena's mind was swirling. Her face had a look John recognized from being in love with a psychiatrist for so many years.

"Depending on what Patch says, I may call him," Marlena offered.

"You miss working and you miss friends, don't you?" John said, with a look Marlena recognized from being in love with a man who had known her well for so many years.

"Christmas was a bit tough," she admitted. "With the kids all doing their own things on the other side of the world and the situation with Charley up in the air…"

Things had been somewhat unsettling since John and Marlena had discovered that Charley Gaines was their biological daughter. She had visited them once since the revelation the previous summer, and while it was a friendly visit, it had been a bit strained. They were all amazed by the genetic traits they shared, from the way Charley's and Marlena's eyes smiled exactly the same way to the way Charley cocked her eyebrow like John when she questioned something. But in essence they were strangers with no shared life experiences to bind them. At least not yet.

"I'm not sure sending that family album for Christmas helped," Marlena added.

"It was a beautiful book and a thoughtful gift," John assured her.

"But since I had one made for each of the kids…it just may have been too pushy."

"Doc, you said yourself that Charley'll reach out to us when and if she wants us in her life," John reminded her.

"That was me being a doctor, not a woman," she admitted.

"And if there is anything you are in spades, it's a woman," he growled sexily.

"I love you," Marlena said, managing a smile.

"And I love nothing more than being with my gorgeous wife, but we can only have so many romantic dinners."

"How am I to take that?" She grimaced.

"Maybe it's time for an adventure."

"Like the helicopter skiing you're determined to try?" Marlena said, tilting her head.

"Why don't you let me surprise you?" John said, cocking his eyebrow in the way that always got her.

12  *JACKSON AND ABBY*

JACKSON DIDN'T NEED LONG TO REALIZE THAT ABBY'S favorite gastro-pub was not the best place to try to extricate himself from his self-inflicted predicament. As they walked into the busy restaurant, he realized they knew a number of people nursing Bloody Marys with their brunch, and the entire staff knew Abby as if she were their sister.

Jackson didn't want to hurt her. He knew the pain of being dumped. It had only happened once, but the memory still lingered.

"Kenny," Abby said to the busy waiter, who lit up when he saw her.

"Right on time for your reservation," he lied as he escorted them to the only open table.

Abby didn't need reservations most anywhere. And not because of the guests she did or didn't bring into the restaurant—it was because of the way she cared about the staff as people.

"How was your New Year?" she asked as she and Jackson were seated near the window overlooking the street.

"Not as good as yours, I'd say," Kenny commented as she flicked the fingers on her left hand. "How many carats? And I assume it's from you," he said wide-eyed as he handed Jackson a menu.

"Four…and yes," Jackson answered with a wan smile.

"Ramos Fizz?" Kenny asked Abby, knowing her favorite drink.

"Absolutely," she said, smiling. "Are you still serving breakfast?"

"Until noon on holidays, and always for you." Kenny winked. "She's a favorite of ours, you know," he said to Jackson. "And not just because she's a great tipper."

Abby was known for her generosity. She felt good service deserved to be recognized.

"A Negroni for my future husband?" Abby asked.

"Exactly," Jackson said, a bit startled.

"And kippers and eggs?" she smiled. "Poached easy?"

"Exactly," Jackson repeated.

"Eggs Benedict Royale for me, Kenny," she added. "And how's Daisy?"

"She has a clean bill of health, thanks for asking."

Kenny's Jack Russell terrier had recently had a suspicious lump removed, and Kenny had been a wreck over it.

"You've got a good one here, Jackson," Kenny said as he left to put in their order.

"He likes you," Jackson said, studying the face he'd come to know so well.

"Christmas was tough for him with his dad gone," Abby said. "Maybe I shouldn't have brought that up."

"I doubt his situation was anything like ours," Jackson sighed. "But I think we held it together pretty well."

Jackson, Chance, and Charley had bonded more strongly than

ever that Christmas, following the death of their parents. It was the three of them against the world, and the boys had tried to keep family traditions intact, especially for Charley. Though both brothers had eschewed their religious upbringing, they went to St. Paul's Christmas Eve festal carol service with their sister. The three then spent the night at Jackson's and exchanged gifts in their pj's on Christmas morning.

"You know you can talk to me about anything," Abby offered. "Especially now," she continued, indicating the exquisitely cut ring. "You realize it fits perfectly."

"Um-hmm," Jackson nodded.

"I promise you I will do everything in my power to make you happy, Jackson. I've never felt this loved."

The look in her eyes told him that was true. And to his utter and total surprise, he'd never felt this loved, either.

"One Ramos Fizz and a Negroni," Kenny said, interrupting the moment as he set the drinks in front of them.

"Thanks." Abby smiled warmly and lifted her glass. "To us being the most envied couple in town."

Jackson slowly lifted his tumbler and clinked her frothy libation. He was getting more confused by the minute. He was used to women coming in and out of his life. Yet since his parents died, Abby had been there for him every minute. Had he been so absorbed with his own problems that he had neglected to see just how special she was? And had he come to depend on her warmth and compassion more than he'd expected to?

Abby took a long sip from her glass as she slipped off her sheepskin boot.

Jackson reacted, startled as Abby ran her bare foot up his pant leg and rested it in his lap. He gasped and his eyes widened.

"How hungry are we?" Abby asked with just the right hint of seduction in her voice.

Jackson thrust out his hand as Kenny passed their table. "Could we get our order to go?"

∞

The remains of their brunch sat on the table next to the bed as Abby rolled off Jackson. They'd had nearly two hours of wild sex, and both were giddy and exhausted.

Suddenly they heard a sound. "Well, hello, Abby," Chance said from the open doorway to Jackson's bedroom. He was carrying two large bags from Harrods. "Lovely to see you."

"You, too," Abby murmured, mortified, as she pulled the covers over her head.

Chance could see his mother's diamond still on her ring finger.

"Charley?" Jackson asked.

"Right here, big brother," Charley answered as she passed behind Chance. "Things going well?"

"Actually," Jackson admitted, confused about it himself, "they couldn't be better."

"Sis is leaving in less than two hours," Chance offered, giving his brother a puzzled look. "You two might want to come up for air."

Chance pulled the bedroom door closed and followed Charley into her beautifully appointed bedroom looking across to Princes Gate, the massive complex that was once home to American ambassadors, including Joseph Kennedy.

"Abby's still wearing the ring," Chance said with a lilt in his voice.

"This time, getting it back might not be so easy," Charley offered. "Maybe it's best I'll be out of their hair for a while."

"How long will you be gone?" Chance asked as he started to help her pack.

Charley stammered, "I'm not really sure."

"No, really, how long will you be gone?" he repeated as he emptied the Harrods bag.

"I didn't ask."

Chance was dumbfounded. "You didn't ask?"

"It all happened so fast. And the photographer is so well respected that I just said yes. I have a passport and the time, and having this on my CV...well, I couldn't say anything else."

"You didn't ask." Charley had never been the impulsive type, so Chance was stunned at her lack of information. But all three of the Gaines siblings had been thrown off their pins by their father's betrayal. And though they seldom discussed it, they were more protective of each other than ever.

"You're going halfway around the world—" he cautioned.

"Halfway down the world," she interrupted. "But I need this, Chance, maybe the way we all need change right now. I'll be fine," she assured him. "Really."

The moment was broken as Jackson and a flushed Abby entered. She was now in her skinny jeans and one of Jackson's shirts.

"Hey," Abby said.

"Hey," Charley answered.

"I guess you heard," Abby offered.

"I did. Well, we both did," Charley replied, trying to sound as positive as she could under the circumstances.

"I will always take the best care of your mother's ring. I hope you know that," Abby said with genuine warmth.

"We have no doubt," Chance replied, trying to sound as positive as *he* could under the circumstances.

"I've always wanted a sister, haven't you?" Abby directed that to Charley.

"I—have," Charley answered.

"Now you'll have me and one of my best friends," Abby said, shaking her head in disbelief. "Wow. Will this make me Belle's sister-in-law, too?"

Charley blanched. While Belle Black Brady had been revealed to be Charley's biological sister, Charley still found it hard to think of her as family.

"It's all a bit confusing," Charley said as she looked to her brother.

"Can I tell her myself about this, or do you want to?" Abby asked.

"What do you think's best, Jackson?" Charley asked, trying to give him an out if he wanted one.

"Whatever," is all he could muster.

"I guess this is congratulations, then?" Charley said, trying not to make it sound like a question.

"Thanks, Sis," he answered, trying not to make that sound like a question.

"You're welcome," she sighed. "Now, if you'll excuse me, I've got to finish packing."

"Where are you going?" Abby asked.

"I guess you and Jackson had other things to discuss, but I'm going to South Africa," Charley told her.

"I'm jealous," Abby responded. "I lived down there for a while."

"You did?" Jackson responded.

"There's a lot you don't know about me," Abby replied with a smile. "My grandfather has a medical clinic down there in a little town called Hoedspruit. In fact, my dad's brother, Steve, is there, too. Where are you going? Cape Town?"

Charley just stared at her blankly.

Instead, Chance chimed in.

"She didn't ask."

"Are you sure about this?" Jackson asked, concerned.

"This is a major photo shoot with the best in the business," Charley answered. "What could go wrong?"

13  *SCARLETT*

SCARLETT HAD AN EGO WORSE THAN SUPERMODEL LINDA Evangelista, who was once quoted as saying, "We don't get out of bed for less than ten thousand dollars a day." And her temper was more volatile than Naomi Campbell's. But with jobs few and far between lately, one would have expected she'd have learned to be more humble, more considerate. Unfortunately, she hadn't.

When she sauntered in nearly two hours late for her massage and facial, her attitude didn't endear her to anyone.

"I'm looking for the spa," she said with a look of disdain. The hotel was known for its location and club, and the spa was smaller than she'd expected.

"Take a seat while you wait, Miss O'Hara," the petite blonde behind the counter said.

Me, wait? Scarlett thought.

A chunky American of about fifty was waiting for a body wrap and leaned over to Scarlett. "Some supermodel is getting an extra half hour," the woman sighed. "As if she needed it."

Scarlett realized the woman didn't recognize her, which was good. Sort of.

"You should try the antiaging facial," the woman continued. "Really hydrating."

"Thanks for the tip," Scarlett said as she sank into the lounge chair.

Thanks a heap, she thought.

The door to the facial room opened, and a stunning blonde exited.

"That was really wonderful," the blonde said with a lovely lilt in her voice.

Even from where Scarlett was sitting, she could see that the girl's lips were plump and her teeth as white as snow.

Wonderful, Scarlett said to herself, mocking the beauty.

Wait, Scarlett thought, does she have an accent?

The girl turned to head to the lockers, and Scarlett could see she was more radiant than ever. "Scarlett O'Hara?" the girl asked, stopping in her tracks. "I'm Brigitta. We're shooting together in South Africa."

Just friggin' wonderful! Scarlett screamed in her head.

"Great to meet you," she lied.

"You're Scarlett O'Hara?" the tourist asked as her eyes lit up.

Great, she knows me, Scarlett thought.

"I used to be a big fan," the woman added. "Could I have your autograph?"

"I've never given autographs," Scarlett sniped and strode into the massage room.

The room fell totally silent except for the gently splashing Zen waterfall.

Brigitta grimaced. "Well, this should be fun."

14  *KAYLA AND PATCH*

KAYLA COULD SEE THE PURPLES, GOLDS, AND ORANGES OF the South African sunset, especially dramatic after the summer thunderstorm, through the massive kitchen window in front of her as she cooked. She was preparing an early dinner for her and Steve. It wasn't even six o'clock, but as parents of a two-and-a-half-year-old, they had schedules that had changed drastically since their early days together.

Kayla's parents owned The Brady Pub, one of the most popular gathering spots in Salem, and she'd learned to cook at her mother's knee. Her family was the salt of the earth, and as with so many others, they had their holiday traditions. Even on the other side of the world, those traditions were sacrosanct. New Year's Day for the Bradys meant corned beef and cabbage with boiled potatoes.

"Smells amazing, Sweetness," Steve said as he entered, returning from his meeting with Bill.

"I should have had you invite Bill," she realized. "There's enough for an army here."

"Leftovers for days," Steve said as he picked a piece of the succulent beef from the plate.

"And it'll bring us the good luck it's meant to bring," Kayla said, smiling.

"Let's hope so," Steve answered. With what he'd just learned from Bill, he suspected they were going to need it.

"That sounded ominous," she said. She retrieved two intricately hand-painted African ceramic dinner plates and a child's plate for Joe, all of which had been given to them by one of the many grateful villages.

"As beautiful as everything is in our little cocoon here," Steve said, indicating their home, "we can't deny South Africa's got problems."

Okay, he said to himself, that certainly isn't a lie.

"Which is why we're here," Kayla answered, interrupting his thought. She knew every inflection of Steve's voice, and her antennae went up. "Is there something you're trying to tell me?"

Steve's gaze met hers. He had promised Bill he wouldn't worry Kayla. And if the years had proven anything, it was that Steve was a man of his word.

Besides, this wouldn't be forever.

Fortunately for both of them, the moment was interrupted as Joe came bounding out of his room.

"Dinner!"

"And hello to you, Bud," Steve said with a bit of relief as the towhead ran to the table.

"Hi, Pop." Joe beamed as he climbed into the booster seat on one of the chairs.

"Man hugs?" Steve asked his son, who was the latest joy in his life.

Joe extended his chubby arms to his father for a big hug. "I love you."

"Me, too…and?"

Joe gave his dad a high five with his left hand, a high five with his right, and then clapped three times and saluted. Steve responded in kind.

Kayla couldn't help but smile. This was family. Her family. Her men. They were away from the day-to-day world their friends knew and were bonding in a way most would not understand.

"Corned beef and cabbage?" Kayla asked Joe, knowing he was not fond of most vegetables.

"Potatoes!" Joe beamed.

"Okay, for today, just potatoes," Kayla agreed.

Steve popped open two bottles of beer and poured them into glasses as Kayla filled their plates.

"And everything's good with Bill?" she asked nonchalantly.

"He apologized," Steve said honestly.

"And butter!" Joe chimed in as he looked as his plate.

Kayla studied her husband. She knew him well after all these years, and if he had something he felt he needed to tell her, she knew he would do so eventually.

"Butter!" was Kayla's answer.

She loaded up Joe's potatoes with the DairyBelle butter Joe loved and watched him dig in.

"To the New Year," Kayla said as she raised her tall glass to her husband.

"To the New Year," Steve answered.

As they clinked glasses, both knew something was not being said. But both also knew this was not the time to discuss it.

15  *CHARLEY*

"You sure you have everything?" Abby asked.

Charley was now dressed in a pair of white cotton OMG drawstring pants, a soft-as-velvet cream-colored tee, and white leather slip-ons with an ivory cashmere pashmina draped over her shoulders.

"If I don't, I'm screwed," Charley laughed. "The game farms are not the place to fill in your wardrobe."

The upbeat atmosphere in Jackson's flat was palpable. It had been a while since the Gaines siblings had had such a diversion. Both Jackson and Chance had been stunned when the world branded them as pariahs. There had been a time when the Donald Trumps of the world could go bankrupt twice and still reign supreme. The celebrity cache meant something. But the times they were a-changin'. There were now so many unemployed financial gurus and attorneys who had tanked in the global recession that the job market was flooded with more than capable and less than astronomically expensive talent.

The Gaines brothers were hanging on by the proverbial thread.

"Are you bringing your Hasselblad?" Chance asked.

"I am a very lowly assistant on this shoot, and all I'm looking for is a credit," Charley reminded her savvy brother. "I'm bringing lightweight summer clothes, mosquito repellent, malaria tablets, and a positive attitude."

"It's why we love you," Jackson added.

The buzzer rang from downstairs, and Jackson answered.

"The car is here for Ms. Gaines," the disembodied voice told him.

"Oh, Lord, wish me luck," Charley gasped.

She slipped out of her loafers, tipped her toes into white OMG sheepskin-lined boots, and then shrugged into a camel, triple-ply, cashmere, hooded floor-length coat. It would be nearly one hundred degrees in South Africa, but it was still nearly freezing in London.

∞

Charley was accustomed to being around international celebrities from Brad Pitt to Prince William and was never rattled. But sitting this close to Vince Castle? They were barely into the Knightsbridge traffic when her hands started to shake.

"You okay?" He smiled.

"Just—cold," she lied.

"Tomorrow afternoon you may be wishing you were." He smiled again.

"I hear it's spectacular down there. It's the one place my mother was dying to go...before she died." Charley looked away as the reality washed over her. "Sorry, this happens to me from time to time."

"My mother died when I was ten," Vince told her. "I get it."

"I'm sorry," Charley said.

"Time's a pretty good healer," Vince said warmly as he put his hand on hers in a gentle, comforting manner. "Keeping busy helps, too."

"I guess that's one reason I jumped at this job," she admitted.

"And I thought it was my charming smile that seduced you."

You do have a charming smile, she thought.

"But don't let it fool you," he added. "Once we're on the clock, I'll make the most savage lions around us look like kittens."

"I get that," she nodded.

"Your job, should you wish to accept it, and you already did, is to anticipate my every move."

Is that his hand on mine? she realized. But before she could react, he pulled it away.

"I really do get it," she said with a smile. "From making sure your alarm is set to your phone being charged to the position of your bounce light, should you need it."

"Nice," he said, smiling. "I knew you were the right girl for the job."

"About the job," she asked cautiously. "I have absolutely no details about it. But you know that, I guess."

Vince reached into a Louis Vuitton duffel at his feet and pulled out a two-inch-thick binder labeled "The Look."

Charley started to open it, but he stopped her.

"You'll have plenty of time on the plane to go over the details," he reminded her. "Eleven hours to Johannesburg."

"If anyone understands budgets and scheduling, I do," Charley assured him. After all, she had been at her mother's side at every OMG fashion shoot since she was a toddler.

She slipped the binder into the oversized OMG lambskin handbag that held all of her essentials, next to a book wrapped with a simple ribbon. Vince noticed the book.

"Not sure you'll have time for heavy reading material," he said, smiling.

"It was a Christmas gift," Charley offered and then hesitated. "Long story."

The moment was broken as the driver hit the brakes to avoid running into an unruly pair of tourists who had stumbled into the street. The tires screeched as Vince's arm immediately blocked Charley from being thrown forward into the back of the front seat.

"Thanks," Charley gasped.

"We've got precious cargo here, mate," Vince called to the driver. "Let's get there in one piece."

Lion, kitten, or viper? Charley wondered, as she glanced at the man who could change her career in a heartbeat.

Then she caught herself. *Viper? Where did that image come from? Why would I think that?*

16   *MARLENA AND JOHN*

MARLENA SAT AT THE DESK IN THE MASTER BEDROOM AND hung up her iPhone. She'd spent three glorious hours speaking to her children, who were scattered around the world. Being in Lausanne, Switzerland, Marlena was anywhere from two hours to seven hours ahead of them, and the time difference could be a bit disconcerting. She wished she could talk to her friends in Salem, too, but it was late, late night in the United States, so she would have to wait until late afternoon to connect with anyone.

She sat back and looked around the empty room. John had been predictably absent since his offer to surprise her with an adventure. Knowing John, that could mean anything from a romantic dinner in the vineyards to an impromptu visit to the devastatingly beautiful Greek island of Santorini. If being confined to bed for nearly two years had done anything for her husband, it had been to ignite his already white-hot passion for the unpredictable.

Then, as she cradled her chin in her hands, she noticed something that didn't please her.

"Is that for us?" she asked.

It was a helicopter. And it was headed straight for Maison du Noir.

"Don't be pissed at me, Doc," she heard from the ceiling-high doorway behind her.

She turned and there was John, dressed and ready to go.

"A helicopter from door to ski lift?" she asked with an arched look.

Her voice was drowned out as the A-Star B2 chopper whirred past the enormous window and landed on an open pad next to the vineyard.

"Would I do that to you?" John grinned.

It was the same sexy, funny, Cheshire cat grin that he knew melted her the minute he used it.

"As long as *you're* happy," she answered. And the truth was that she meant it. John had been through such torture in his life that the least she could do was let him enjoy this freedom.

"Just let me pack," she said, smiling. "I assume you have the ski gear arranged."

"The chopper's packed with everything we need," he dodged. "Top to tail."

"Let me get my makeup and—"

He cut her off. "I said everything, and I meant everything. No need to get anything but your beautiful butt out the door."

"The new toothpaste…?"

John rolled his eyes.

"My eye mask…"

John took her hand and guided her out of the room.

"Sunscreen! The glare on my skin from the snow is—"

"Am I going to have to cover you with kisses to get you to *ferme* that *bouche*?" he laughed.

"Would that be so bad…" She giggled coyly.

"There'll be plenty of time for that on the plane," he answered. "Now move it, Sister!"

"Yes, sir!" Marlena smiled as she finally got into the spirit of things.

Wait a minute, did he say "plane"? she asked herself as they headed down the winding staircase.

∞

The flight in the state-of-the-art helicopter was as smooth as the whipped cream on the Irish Coffees John and Marlena sipped as they flew over Lake Geneva.

Marlena couldn't resist dipping her finger into the white froth, dabbing it on the tip of John's nose, and then kissing it off.

John returned the gesture in kind.

Though being passionate was a bit awkward while wearing the headphones required in the helicopter, they were in sync and connected perfectly. This trip was starting off well for both of them.

"I think this is my favorite time of the day," Marlena sighed as she looked out the window.

The sun was just setting, creating streaks of vibrant coral and peach across the deep blue of the winter sky. The vistas in front of them were dazzling. "I love seeing the lights flickering on as families are settling in for the evening," she continued.

"We'll be seeing that all the way to the Geneva airport," John offered pointedly.

"You did say 'plane,' didn't you," she confirmed as she looked him square in the eye.

"When?" He shrugged as though he had no idea what she meant.

"Where are we skiing?" Marlena asked.

"We'll be landing in five minutes," the pilot interrupted through their headsets.

"Does it really matter as long as we're together?" John answered.

Marlena was getting more curious by the second.

The helicopter set down at the private jet terminal of the Geneva airport, next to a Gulfstream V superjet.

"John?" was all Marlena could say.

"Nice, huh?" was all he answered.

As they boarded the plane, Marlena's mind was spinning.

"Who are we traveling with?" she asked. It was a logical question since the "GV," one of the fastest private jets in the world, could hold eighteen passengers.

"It's just you and me," he smiled.

"John…" she gasped.

"You've already said that," he countered.

A strikingly handsome, uniformed flight attendant appeared from the back galley holding a silver tray with Dom Pérignon Rosé, strawberries, and crème fraîche.

"Doctor Evans, Mr. Black." The tanned thirty-year-old Norwegian smiled.

"You can call us Marlena and John," John said as he took the champagne flutes from the tray.

"Randy," the attendant said, smiling. "We'll be ready to take off in about fifteen minutes. Let me know if you need anything, anything at all. We're fully stocked according to your requests, and I'm at your beck and call."

"Thanks," John answered.

"I have a question," Marlena said as she took her glass from John. "How long is our flight time?"

"Approximately eleven hours." Randy smiled as he put the silver tray on the linen-covered table that had been set up mid-cabin. "Cheers."

Marlena stared at the husband she adored and who, since his recovery, was especially full of surprises.

"Eleven hours…?"

"I knew you were worried about Bill Horton. So I thought maybe you'd want to see in person." John smiled warmly.

Marlena was thunderstruck. And speechless.

"Amazing what you can arrange with a few phone calls these days," he added.

"Do Patch and Kayla even know?" she asked with a hint of trepidation.

"Everyone who needs to know does," he answered. "And they asked us to stay with them, but I thought being in the house with a two-year-old wasn't really the kind of vacation we needed. I was able to snag a suite at a game farm called the Royal Londolani."

"Oh, my," Marlena gasped.

"Not far from them and the clinic, from what I hear."

"It's gorgeous. It opened just before I went down there to volunteer."

"Nothing but the best for my lady," he said, smiling.

"Have I told you how much I adore you?" Marlena asked as she stared into John's clear blue eyes.

"You can always show me after we take off," he answered. Those same blue eyes were lit with the passion he'd felt for her since the day he'd met her more than twenty-five years earlier. "I made sure this jet has very private berths."

∞

When the plane reached cruising altitude, John refilled the two flutes of champagne and returned to Marlena on the couch.

"You do think of everything," she cooed as she slid her legs underneath herself, took a sip, and snuggled into John.

"Only the best for my girl," John replied, "and that includes the very best of me, too."

Effortlessly, John set aside his drink and pulled the love of his life onto his lap.

"Let me know if this is one of my best." He grinned slyly and slid his probing tongue into her mouth.

She gasped as John worked his way down her neck with his tongue while he undid the buttons of her blouse and then slid his hand inside to cup her breast.

Her ragged breathing was joined by a groan as John's fingers fondled her.

"I treasure every moment with you, Doc," John breathed. "And making love to you is one of my greatest joys."

"I adore you, John Black," she answered coyly, aware that the flight attendant could appear any moment. "I always have."

She put aside her intoxicating bubbly and slid off John's lap. Then, taking his hand, she led him to that very private berth.

She pushed the call button and Randy appeared.

"Don't worry about us for the rest of the night," she smiled, her eyes sparkling.

"You know where to find me if you need me."

Randy slid the partition closed, and Marlena turned to her admiring husband.

Slowly, she began to peel off the rest of her clothes before returning to kneel at his feet.

Piece by piece, she helped him remove his shirt, slacks, and Calvins, kissing every bit of newly exposed flesh as she did.

"Of all the places we've made love," Marlena acknowledged, "our private times on your plane are some of the most memorable."

John pulled Marlena onto himself on the bed and kissed her with an intensity to match the animal prowess they would soon witness in the Timbavati.

Her fingers were on his chest as John's hands worked themselves into Marlena's hair, tipping her head back slowly to expose her luscious neck. Their bodies joined and began to writhe, first slowly and then with increasing rhythm, as they soared together across the sky.

17  CHARLEY

CHARLEY'S AIRPORT EXPERIENCE AT HEATHROW WASN'T quite the same as the one John and Marlena had experienced in Geneva. Heathrow was always a madhouse, even on New Year's Day. Charley had flown out of the massive airport dozens of times on her trips from her family home in Holland Park to Choate Rosemary Hall, the prestigious prep school in Connecticut from which she'd graduated a year earlier.

When the town car carrying her and Vince pulled up to the gleaming glass-and-steel structure, Charley smiled. Terminal 5 had only been open since 2008, but it was one of her favorites. The days when time spent in an airport was torture were long gone; not only was the futuristic terminal a creative masterpiece, but it had a First Class lounge that was, well, first class.

Their arrival time was perfect. Charley could see that several others from the crew for the shoot were gathered just inside waiting, and they appeared to be the crème de la crème. MAC's brilliant senior makeup artist, Gregory Arlt; hair god Alex Roldan; and über-stylist Rachel Zoe's latest protégée, Ashley

Avignone, were all deep in conversation, along with an already frazzled assistant.

Vince led the way into the terminal as Charley handed their boarding passes to the skycap. It was a quick and simple process, but she could sense Vince's impatience as he waved her inside.

"Everyone, meet my new assistant," Vince stated as she entered, trailing their carry-ons behind her. "Charley Gaines, meet everyone."

Before anyone even had a chance to respond, Vince strode toward the security check-ins.

"Hi, all," is all Charley could get out before falling in step behind him.

"I had better see Blonde, Black, and Red in the lounge," Vince muttered as he scanned the crowd.

I guess this is on-the-clock time, Charley thought to herself.

∞

The First Class lounge, the Concorde Room, was on the far end of the terminal on the upper level, and Charley knew it well. When she entered and saw the polished wood counter with the floor-to-ceiling bar visible behind it, she felt at home.

"Gary," she said to the agent behind the highly polished, burled wood counter.

"Charley, nice to see you. Sorry about—last year?" he added with a bit of hesitation. Charley had found that people who knew about her family crisis often didn't know what to say.

"I'm doing fine," she hedged. "We all are." Then she shifted gears. "We're together," she added as she slid hers and Vince's boarding passes toward him. "Working," she clarified as Gary looked at Vince.

"Come right in…Oh—whoops," he grimaced. "Mr. Castle is fine. But your ticket is economy. You'll have to wait outside," Gary told her reluctantly.

Charley was thrown. She hadn't even looked at her ticket or given it a second thought. She hadn't traveled economy class since she was five. While she didn't consider herself spoiled, this isn't exactly what she had expected.

"Oh," was all she could muster. She turned to Vince, "Vince, I'll be right outsi—"

But Vince had already moved into the lounge and was headed to the bar. From Charley's vantage point, she could see Vince approach three women at the bar. The so-called blonde, black, and red must be the models Vince had hired for the shoot, she figured.

"At least they're here." Charley smiled wanly at the embarrassed desk agent. "The models."

"And only one of them is drunk," Gary said, smiling and tipping his hand to his mouth as Charley made her way out the door.

While passengers passed in and out, Charley waited patiently. When the door was opened a crack, she strained to see Vince but to no avail.

Maybe I should have asked a few questions, she thought.

After about ten minutes, she was startled when the door opened again and Vince exited with the three models in tow.

The young blonde was luminescent, though a bit vacant, and the African-American was radiant. And the redhead? She was not only drunk, she was…*Scarlett O'Hara*, Charley gasped to herself.

Vince put his hand on the small of Scarlett's back and led the wobbly supermodel past Charley, the other models following.

"Everyone, meet my new assistant," Vince said, echoing his earlier introduction as they walked past her.

"Charley," she offered.

"Brigitta." The blonde nodded sweetly, and then hiccupped.

"I'm Nikki." The raven-haired beauty smiled as they moved on in sync.

"Don't I know you?" Scarlett slurred as she checked out Charley through her haze.

"Not really," Charley said, trying to keep from stirring the pot.

You knew me when I was nine, Charley mused. When you dumped my brother.

18  KAYLA AND PATCH

STEVE WAS NURSING A BEER IN FRONT OF THE TV, WATCHING THE Rose Bowl game from Pasadena, when a news bulletin broke in.

"Police have arrested eleven suspected members of a major rhino-poaching ring. They have been linked to a number of incidents, including one last night in which five rhino were apparently killed in the Timbavati, their horns severed."

"Whew!" Kayla said as she entered from Joe's room, interrupting the broadcast. "Joe is sleeping like a baby."

"Shhhh!" Steve said, silencing her.

Kayla froze in her tracks as the news account continued.

"According to Johannesburg police, the suspects include two well-respected Kruger National Park rangers and a game farmer. They are expected to appear in court on Wednesday to face charges including assault, defeating the ends of justice, fraud, corruption, malicious injury to property, and illegal possession of weapons and ammunition. It is the largest arrest made since the war against the poachers escalated in the past six months. We will bring you more details as we receive them…"

The bulletin ended and the football game returned to the screen just as Wisconsin scored a touchdown.

"I didn't mean to shush you, Sweetness. I'm sorry," Steve answered as he was pulled out of his reverie.

"Don't be," she answered. "It's still so amazing to me that all that danger is really out there." She pointed to the vastness that was just outside their doors.

"Try being a guy wanting to make sure his wife and son are as safe as they can be."

"If I were a rhino, maybe you'd need to worry," Kayla answered. "But these despicable creatures couldn't care less about us, unless we get in their way. All they care about is the money."

"You do feel safe here, don't you?" Steve asked.

"With you by my side, absolutely," Kayla offered gently. "If we didn't need to get Joe back to the States for school when he's older, I'd live here forever."

"For the people," Steve said. He knew his wife and how committed she was to offering aid to the thousands of villagers.

"They need us," she said, agreeing.

"But you are happy about John and Marlena coming in?" He grinned.

"I am *so* excited to see them," she admitted.

"I know you are, Sweetness," Steve said.

"Aren't you?" she said, intrigued by his tone.

He was actually torn; he was excited to see them, of course, but he had a strong feeling that the secret he was keeping was about to get bigger. Since Bill didn't want Kayla to know about the likely fate of the clinic, he would most likely keep John and Marlena in the dark, too. Bill was a man of tremendous pride, and a handout was the last thing he'd ask for.

"It'll be great to see them, yes," Steve nodded.

John and Steve had been two of the strongest, most romantic and charismatic men Salem had ever seen. They were both alpha males on the opposite ends of the spectrum. Steve "Patch" Johnson was the quintessential bad boy from the wrong side of the tracks, and John was the sexy, sophisticated stranger with a past more convoluted than Jason Bourne's. The two men had butted heads on more than one occasion, but their respect for each other had never wavered.

"Amazing what money can do, isn't it," Kayla said, more as a statement than a question. "I can't even imagine what a private jet costs from Geneva down here. But it's their money, and whatever makes them happy makes me happy."

Steve looked at the woman who'd seen him through more than a life's worth of trials. Her goodness and sincerity melted his heart.

"I like to see that smile, baby," Steve said.

"I like your smile, too," she responded. "And I know that whatever had you distracted earlier is not doing anything to help."

"Not really," he said, reacting to her tone and glancing at her sideways.

"Will this?" she asked, picking up the remote and clicking off the TV. Then she moved to the music system near their deck windows and turned it on.

Steve couldn't help but smile as he heard "The Lady in Red" filter through the speakers. Since the day it was released, it had remained their song.

Kayla was silhouetted against the Southern Hemisphere's unpredictable night sky as she slipped her white cotton robe from her shoulders. Underneath was a lacy, short, red silk nightie that skimmed her frame.

Steve rose from his chair and joined her.

"You do know how to make a man smile," he said, his voice hoarse as he pulled her close.

Kayla melted into his arms as they moved as one in the moonlight.

Despite whatever mystery and danger and life lurked just outside, their own primal dance had begun.

19 FLYING HIGH

THE SUN WAS FILTERING THROUGH THE CRACK IN THE window next to Charley's row on the Boeing 744. She sat dozing in her middle seat with the project binder still open on her lap.

"Hey," Charley heard as a slim hand jostled her awake.

Her eyes fluttered open to see Scarlett leaning across the annoyed stylist's assistant sitting next to her.

"Hi," Charley muttered, half awake.

"You are Jackson Gaines' sister!" Scarlett said in a voice loud enough to wake everyone around her.

"I am." Charley half smiled. "Does Vince need me?" she asked quietly.

"How is that gorgeous brother of yours?" Scarlett asked, totally ignoring the stares from the grumbling passengers.

"Engaged," Charley answered. "And I think you're being a little—loud?" she whispered.

"Ma'am," Scarlett heard from behind her. She turned to face a lovely flight attendant of about thirty. "You need to get back to your seat."

"'Ma'am'?" Scarlett bristled.

"Please," the attendant offered pleasantly.

"I'm just talking to my friend," Scarlett said, wide-eyed.

"We'll be landing in thirty minutes, and we need to make sure everyone's in their seats," the attendant said, gently putting her hand on Scarlett's arm to guide her. "This way."

"Don't touch me!" Scarlett bristled, stepping back and knocking a cup of coffee out of the hand of a passenger in the middle section.

"Jeez Louise!" the passenger grumbled.

"Ma'am...*Miss*...please," the attendant snapped.

"If you hadn't pushed me, that wouldn't have happened!" Scarlett shrieked.

Charley stuffed the binder into her satchel and climbed over the girl next to her, trying to quell the situation.

"Scarlett, let's get you back where you belong," Charley begged. "We're really sorry, everyone."

"We?" Scarlett snapped. Then she noticed that passengers up and down the narrow rows were all staring back at the commotion. "What are you all looking at?" she shouted. Then she glared at Charley. "And sit yourself down."

This really is not going well, Charley thought.

"Excuse me," Scarlett barked at the attendant.

As the attendant plastered herself against one of the seats, Scarlett strode by. "And that was *your* fault, not mine!"

Charley sighed and climbed back into her seat.

None of them noticed a girl in the bulkhead filming a video of the entire tirade on her iPhone.

∞

It was six-thirty in the morning when they finally landed. After going through customs and security in Jo'burg, they had a two-hour layover before climbing onto a South African Airways flight for Hoedspruit. Fortunately, the airport's First Class lounge had been voted one of the best in the world, and the entire team was invited in for breakfast.

The moment Charley walked in the lounge, she could see that Vince was not happy. He was reading something on his phone as she approached.

"How did this happen?" Vince asked Charley without even looking up.

"Beg your pardon?" she asked sweetly.

"The client is now pissed that I hired Scarlett."

"Why?"

"Her meltdown on the plane is already online," Vince said as he showed it to Charley.

"What?" Charley was dumbstruck.

"Spectator.com," Vince said.

Charley's heart sank.

"There are times when gossip is good, but this ain't one of 'em," Vince added. "See if you can find out who gave it to them. I want whoever's responsible fired."

20  *TOM-ALI CLINIC*

ON THE FIRST DAY THE CLINIC WAS FULLY OPEN IN THE NEW year, a line of Xsoha men, women, and children stood outside. Some had traveled from their nearest rural villages by minibus, some on bicycles, and others by foot for the free medical services they'd come to depend on. They waited patiently outside in the dense heat while Bill and Cornelius prepared the exam rooms for the general physicals and the free TB and HIV tests.

"How many are out there?" Bill asked as Cornelius brought boxes of condoms from the storage room. The tribesmen had once believed that the white man was trying to keep them from procreating, not saving their lives, but now they were finally accepting distribution of both male and female condoms.

"Looks to be about fifty," Cornelius answered as he set the boxes on the counter.

"And we got our supply of ARVs?"

The government had been providing the antiviral HIV drugs to the private clinics as part of a massive drive to stem the tide of the deadly disease, which was crippling the country.

"Last Tuesday," Cornelius answered. "I told you last week."

"Right," Bill answered, though in truth he had no memory of that. "When's Kayla due in?"

"You asked me to tell her we could handle this morning because she had to cover New Year's Eve."

"I did?" Bill asked.

"She'll be here around noon to head over to the weavers," Cornelius answered. "You okay?"

Bill merely nodded.

A lithe young girl of about fifteen came from the back with a large pitcher of iced tea.

"For you," she said simply. She wore a colorful red top and skirt with bracelets up both forearms and at her ankles.

"Thank you, Beauty," Bill said with a smile. The girl, whose name actually was Beauty, had volunteered to help in whatever way she could after Kayla nursed her mother back to health from a severe bout of malaria.

Cornelius took three tumblers and poured each of them a glass of the cold liquid. One had a worn, etched "H" in gold, and he handed that one to Bill.

"And thank you," Bill said as he took his drink and downed it.

"Should we get started?" Cornelius asked.

"One thing first," Bill said. "I'm sorry about the problem with the van the other night."

Cornelius was circumspect since Beauty was nearby. "I put the new tire on my personal credit card. And got a spare."

"You didn't tell Kayla, did you?"

"No. Nor did I tell her that while I was out there I saw one of the dead rhino that was part of that bloodbath."

"Wow. At least they got those guys," Bill said, shaking his head. "Rangers and even an owner. Unbelievable."

"One of those guys used to hang out at the Safari Club. I used to toss a few back with him. Seemed like a good guy," Cornelius said. "Guess he thought all that cash was worth the risk."

"Guess so," Bill said, his mind reeling. His own financial pressures were weighing on him heavily. He wiped his brow.

"You sure you're up to this?" Cornelius asked.

"Absolutely. We have a job to do."

Bill nodded to Beauty, who stood waiting for their instructions. Her English was good enough that she served not only as an aide but also as a translator for patients who only knew their native Xhosa or Sotho.

"Remind them to be patient. We'll make sure we have time for them all."

"I will, Dr. Bill," she said, smiling. "Thank you."

Beauty bowed lightly and went out the front door as the light from the summer sun poured in. As she guided in the first patients, a mother with two small children, Bill could see two top-of-the-line Londolani Rovers pass down the bumpy road toward the game farms.

21  *CHARLEY*

BECAUSE IT WAS MIDDAY, THE DRIVE TO THE GAME FARM from Hoedspruit airport was extremely hot. It was the height of South African summer, after all.

The countryside was also serene and nearly indescribably beautiful. With a climate that often mirrored Tuscany or the Santa Barbara coast in California, the terrain included soft rolling hills, soaring mountains, and dense vegetation due to the unpredictable summer rains. But there were no skyscrapers, electrical wires, telephone lines, or billboards to mar the view. It was nature at its most perfect.

"Where are all the animals?" Scarlett called to the game ranger, Ben, from her high third-row seat in the Rover.

While they'd glimpsed an occasional wildebeest, impala, and what might have been zebra through the dense brush, the sightings were minimal.

"Good question. Anyone want to guess the answer?" the khaki-clad thirty-year-old asked. Though an apprentice ranger, he was one of the most knowledgeable in the Timbavati and liked to encourage his guests to learn.

"I think it's because of the heat," Charley offered. She wasn't used to being low man on any totem pole, so she had no qualms about speaking up. "They're buried deep in the mud or the bush."

"Exactly! They are where we'd like to be right now. Taking naps in whatever shade they can find," the khaki-clad ranger offered. "And there's plenty. That's why our drives are at sunset or sunrise," he added.

"Cool!" Brigitta piped up.

"The only time it is." Ben smiled at the flaxen-haired beauty. He liked Brigitta's youthful enthusiasm.

Scarlett didn't. "Wait," she blurted. "What time is the game ride?"

"There's one every night at sunset, but we'll be shooting in the lodge starting at six so we're going to miss it. Then there's dinner so you can get to sleep early. Your call time is 3:00 a.m. for the five-thirty ride," Charley told her.

Scarlett fell back in her seat. "And for so much money," she grumbled.

The truth was that cover and editorial shoots were not that lucrative in the scheme of things and never had been. They were for the visibility and prestige. True, they could pay upwards of seventy-five thousand dollars, but the modeling megabucks were reserved for endorsements. Bulgari, Christian Dior, Victoria's Secret. The current and only super-supermodel, Gisele Bündchen, was worth more than one-hundred-fifty million dollars, but that kind of money was rarer than hen's teeth.

The Rovers turned down a narrow road and within minutes were in front of the open, thatched-roof main hall where six staff members in African regalia were waiting.

Vince was first out of the Rover, with Charley scrambling out right behind him.

"Make sure everyone stays close and heads right into reception," she instructed Kelly, the assistant assigned to the rest of the creative team.

As everyone piled out of the Rover, Charley and Vince headed inside.

Charley was taken aback as she entered. She had been raised by one of the top designers in the world in exquisitely furnished homes in London, Monte Carlo, and Malibu. Her parents both collected art from Picasso to Degas and Rothko. And still she was impressed.

"Mummy would have loved this," Charley gasped as she got her first glimpse of the rich antique chairs, sofas, and tables, as well as Persian carpets and details that perfectly complemented the colonial elegance. To the right, she could glimpse the dining room, with armoires of the finest porcelain, crystal, and silver. A full library was filled with tomes that reached the high-beamed ceilings. This was a place to lose one's self. To escape every problem left back in the real world.

"Charley?" she heard coming from the conversation area behind her.

The voice sounded familiar, and she bristled. Slowly, she turned to see the last people she had expected to run into in South Africa: John and Marlena.

∞

John and Marlena were thunderstruck, particularly Marlena.

"Is it weird to ask what you're doing here?" John asked casually as Charley approached.

"Is it weird to ask what *you're* doing here?" Charley responded with a wry smile. They were all trying to be as casual as possible, but the situation was awkward. Marlena and John had reached out to her with the Christmas gift, and she'd not yet responded.

"We were both restless and have friends in Hoedspruit, actually. Where you landed, I'd guess?" he said, trying to clarify.

"Where'd you land?" Charley asked, surprised.

"There's a private landing strip here," John answered. "We jetted in this morning."

"Excuse me, Mr. Black—Dr. Evans," one of the staff interrupted. "Your ride is ready."

The Rovers were now empty, and one was available for them as the production crew assembled in the nearby lobby.

"Our friends run one of the medical clinics in town," John explained. "Marlena's volunteered there. We're headed there now."

"I'm here working," Charley said, trying to explain.

"On the photo shoot?" John asked. "Impressive. We hear it's a big one."

Charley nodded. She was about to apologize for not calling, but suddenly Vince was right behind her, yelling, "Let's get a move on!"

"Yes, Mr. Castle." She blanched.

"We need to get going," he instructed. "Vince Castle, hello," he said, extending his hand to John.

"John Black," John said, firmly shaking Vince's hand. "And my wife, Marlena Evans."

"You all know each other?" Vince realized.

"It's a long story," Charley interrupted. "We've got a busy shooting schedule. We're here for a photo shoot. But we'll catch up if there's time," she said to John and Marlena.

"Maybe at dinner," John answered. "Doc?"

"Yes, dinner."

"Lovely to see you, Charley," was all Marlena could muster, and she joined John on the way to their transportation.

"Did she ever model?" Vince asked Charley as he watched Marlena go. "She has beautiful bone structure."

"Yes, she does," Charley answered.

"Let's get to our suite," Vince said.

"Of course."

Charley was so shaken by the unexpected encounter with her biological parents on the bottom of the world that what he said took a moment to sink in.

"*Our* suite?" she said, stopping in her tracks.

"Kevin, my assistant, and I always shared a suite so he could keep on top of me." He grinned. "You can handle that, can't you?" he called back to her as he exited.

"I can handle anything," she answered.

And I'll sleep in the bathtub if I have to.

22   MARLENA, JOHN, PATCH, AND KAYLA

JOHN SLIPPED HIS ARM AROUND MARLENA AS THE AIR-conditioned van carried them toward Tom-Ali. Her expression was a mixture of nerves and elation.

"You okay, Doc?" John asked gently.

"I can't believe Charley is here, too. How do things like this happen?" Marlena questioned.

"Are you sorry it did?" John replied.

"Honestly, I'm not sure," she admitted. "Charley has been through so much in the last year. Finding out her father destroyed so many lives with his greed and lying. Her mother being poisoned and being in the car with her when she died." The reminder made Marlena shudder. "Sometimes I think of how Charley could have died in that accident, too…"

"And we'd never have known about her," John said in agreement.

"I feel as responsible for reaching out to her as I do for leaving her alone," Marlena said, her voice choking. "Everyone assumes psychiatrists have all the answers. But that's when we're not emotionally involved, and that's not now."

"We're all human," John said. "Even my gorgeous you."

There was a silence as she leaned against him.

"You know how much I've been wanting some resolution. Truly, John, did you know she'd be here?"

"Doc, how would I have known?" he said sincerely. "I made a few calls yesterday, and this was the only luxury game farm within driving distance of Hoedspruit that had any space. Because of a photo shoot," he added with emphasis. "They promised me it wouldn't be intrusive…and I figured we'd be spending plenty of 'us' time in our amazingly sexy room, so…here we are. Coincidence or fate. I guess that's the real question."

"Of all the places in the world," Marlena said, forcing a smile.

They drove in silence the rest of the trip, resting in the comfort of each other's touch and taking in the glory that surrounded them. They were both a jumble of emotions and thought—excitement, confusion, anticipation, and fear.

~

Hoedspruit had grown since Marlena had last been there, with an added smattering of shops, art galleries, and bars and restaurants. But it was still reminiscent of the small towns so many Americans had once called home. Salem had never been this small or this remote, but something about the friendliness of the people reminded Marlena of the Midwest.

Then she saw Kayla and felt completely at home.

Kayla was standing outside the clinic with several young ebony girls when the Royal Londolani van drove in. She kissed each of the girls warmly on the cheek, and they trotted barefoot down the road before she headed for her friends.

"Steve," she called out excitedly. "They're here!"

They had not seen one another for nearly three years, and the foursome embraced each other warmly.

"So great to see you guys," Kayla said, breaking into her classic bright smile. She and Marlena hugged tightly.

"So much has changed." Marlena smiled. "Except the clinic," she added, unaware of the reason why.

"So this is it," John said, nodding. "I've heard amazing things about the place."

"We're a bit rustic at the moment, but we're getting a complete overhaul in the next few months," Kayla said with a hint of apology. "So the air conditioner's a bit woofy. But come in, come in. And Bill doesn't know you're here."

Cornelius had been replacing meds in a locked cabinet and was startled when the four of them entered.

"Cornelius, these are two of our dearest friends from home," Kayla said enthusiastically. "Marlena Evans and John Black."

Cornelius quickly wiped his hands and extended one to John. "Very pleased to make your acquaintance," he said.

John shook his hand firmly.

"Very nice to meet you," Cornelius said, taking Marlena's hand and tipping his head with a smile.

"Bill about done back there?" Patch asked.

"Just about," Cornelius answered.

"It is still blazing hot out there." Kayla sighed. "Would you like some iced tea while we wait?"

"Sounds good," John said, smiling.

"Four glasses comin' up," Patch offered as he moved to the counter.

"Let me get 'em," Cornelius insisted. "You talk with your friends."

While Cornelius took down the tumblers from the shelf and poured them each a drink, Kayla studied Marlena.

"Want to tell me what's going on?" she asked.

Marlena and John exchanged glances.

"What, are you psychic now?" John questioned, raising his eyebrow.

"Maybe it's spending so much time down here," Kayla answered. "There's a lot of mystical energy around us," she added as she swirled her hands in the air. "Besides, I know that when someone's blinking a lot, it means something. And you, Marlena, were blinking…"

"Charley is at the Royal Londolani on a photo shoot," Marlena admitted. "John said 'coincidence or fate,' and there you go."

Kayla was stunned. She was one of the few people Marlena had confided in about the discovery that Charley was her and John's daughter.

"Well, that does it," Bill was heard saying as he exited the exam room. He was walking out with a forty-year-old African farmworker whose arm was in a sling. "Tell him no heavy lifting…" he said to Beauty. Then he stopped in his tracks. "I must be dreaming!"

"Hi, Bill," Marlena said warmly.

"When, what, how…?" he laughed. He was truly thrilled to see Marlena. He had known her since she'd just graduated from med school and was brought in to counsel distraught Laura, the woman who eventually became Bill's wife.

"It was all very last minute," Marlena said. "Do you know John?"

"Just by reputation," Bill answered. On the few trips he'd taken back to Salem in the last twenty years, they'd never met. He took John's hand. "This is just, well, unbelievable." He turned to Beauty and the patient who were totally confused. "In two weeks I want to see you," he told the patient and held up two fingers.

"Thank you...Dr. Bill," the man said in broken English. "Thank you."

"And thank you, Beauty," Kayla added. "We'll see you day after tomorrow?"

"Yes, most surely," Beauty nodded. Then she headed out the door.

"He's not doing so hot, is he?" John said.

"Forty years old and ravaged by weather and HIV," Bill explained. "Not a bad life span around here." Realizing how that sounded, he shook off the reality of it all.

"You like something cool?" Cornelius asked.

"Yeah, thanks," he answered as Cornelius got a tumbler from the high shelf and poured Bill a long one. "Any chance of our getting dinner?"

John piped in. "We're pretty exhausted, but we thought we'd catch the five-thirty game ride at Londolani. I know Doc wants to spend as much time here as she can in the afternoons, though."

"I was supposed to go to Mapusha today, but birthin' a baby in our parking lot got in my way," Kayla interjected.

"A beautiful little scooter they're naming 'Patch,' by the way," Steve smiled.

"I'd love to come with you," Marlena beamed. "It's been so long since I've been here that I wonder if they'll remember me."

"Who wouldn't remember *that* face, Doc?" John smiled sexily.

"You, too?" Cornelius laughed and indicated Patch and Kayla. "These two are so lovey-dovey it makes your head spin. What's in the water in Salem?"

He was nonchalant and charming as he handed Bill the tumbler with the gold "H."

"Can we talk tonight or have an early lunch tomorrow?" Marlena asked Bill, who was just finishing a sip of tea. "Just the two of us. We have so much to catch up on."

Bill lowered the glass and caught Marlena's look. He'd seen that look many times, not only from Marlena but from his ex who was also a psychiatrist.

"Sure. Just the two of us," he said calmly. But his hand began to shake.

You already know I'm falling apart, don't you?

23 *CHARLEY, ABBY, AND JACKSON*

RAISED AS THE DAUGHTER OF AN INFAMOUS BILLIONAIRE, Charley had seen almost everything. But she was still quite impressed by their suite.

They were escorted there by Tuma, the Sotho staff member who'd been assigned to them. Accessed by elevated walkways to ensure the guests stayed on clear paths and out of the way of the nature that enveloped them, the suites were massive and beautifully appointed.

"Not bad, eh?" Vince smiled as they entered.

"Mind-blowing actually." Charley said, smiling.

"And yes, there are two bedrooms." Vince grinned. "Relieved?"

"And why would I have to worry about you, Mr. Castle?" Charley answered directly.

"Because my reputation precedes me?" he said with his eyes twinkling, making Charley a bit nervous.

"Your bags are already in your closets, sir." The gentle but beefy Sotho nodded as he indicated the larger room. "As are yours, Miss," he added, nodding to the second room. "Whatever you need, just dial seven on the desk phone and you can reach me."

"The tips will be when we leave." Vince directed that to Tuma in a somewhat dismissive tone. "Now we've got work to do."

"Remember to never leave the room without someone with you," Tuma reminded them both firmly. "A ranger at a nearby camp was killed by a lion three weeks ago when he ventured to another bungalow on his own."

"Guess he should have remembered his gun," Vince said cavalierly.

"We'll be gathering in the main lounge at five for cocktails before tonight's game drive," Tuma said, ignoring the comment. "If you wish to be there, just let us know."

"We're working, pal," Vince said curtly. "But when we need you, we'll dial seven."

Tuma nodded and left quietly.

There was the ping of a text on Vince's phone. He glanced at it and then put his phone on the table.

"The client again…still not happy," he said with purpose. "Too bad we're busy. And I'm gonna take a dip in the pool and grab a shower before we get to it. Oh, and enough of that Mr. Castle crap. Mr. Castle is my grandfather."

Charley nodded, "Got it."

"Vince—?"

"Vince," she said with a bit of difficulty. Having been brought up in prep schools, she was accustomed to calling her elders and bosses by their formal names. But he was the boss, after all, so "Vince" it would be.

"And get on that Internet disaster," Vince called to her as he disappeared into his room.

∞

Charley was remarkably impressed with her room as she entered. High-beamed ceilings with wrought-iron chandeliers and a ceiling fan. Comfortable down sofas covered with heavy white cotton covers and a beautiful king-sized bed with four posters. And a sheer white canopy as protection from flying insects, of which there were plenty. Africa is gorgeous, she mused, but nature still reigns.

Charley put her OMG handbag on the dark wood desk and removed the production binder. She also pulled out the bound album she'd brought with her.

Her hand lingered on the Christmas gift she had not yet opened.

First this, she said to herself. Then they show up here?

A beautiful diffused photo of John and Marlena and the words "Our Beautiful Family" graced the cover of the glossy hardcover book.

Charley ran her finger across the title. She felt torn inside.

You're lovely people. But Jackson and Chance are my family.

The moment was broken when she heard a splash in the private pool just outside her room. She looked up to see Vince coming out of the water. Behind him, Charley could see a pair of elephants less than twenty feet from the pool, munching low leaves from one of the sprawling indigenous trees.

Vince shook his long, wavy locks to get them out of his eyes. Then he perched on the side of the pool and gazed out across the high grass rimming the property. He was stark naked. He silently watched the massive, gray hulks that were oblivious to him.

Jolted back to reality, Charley got to work. Fortunately, she'd spent enough time on photo shoots and the beaches in the South of France that Vince's nudity didn't faze her.

Abby was just digging into her wild mushroom gnocchi when her phone rang. Jackson was sitting across the table from her on the terrace at Soho House, one of the few outdoor restaurants in London that was open during the winter when weather permitted. A private club that catered to the media, entertainment, and publishing, Soho House was also popular with the influx of new Chinese multimillionaires who knew how to spend money. They loved to entertain high-profile clients, so the place was always good for an item or two for Spectator.com.

The phone kept ringing. Jackson gave his fiancée a look that said, "Do you have to answer?"

"It's my biz," she responded, grimacing as she took the phone from her bag. She smiled when she saw who it was.

"Charley, hi."

Jackson looked at Abby quizzically. "My Charley?" he mouthed. She nodded.

"Abby, how's it going?"

"I'm at Soho House with your brother who is fab-u-lous, and work is getting crazed now that the holidays are over. You have no idea how many celebrities get married or break up on Christmas and New Year. Probably just for the publicity, but all publicity's good, as they say."

"Not here they don't," Charley said seriously.

"O-kay. How's it going for you then?" Abby asked perplexed.

Jackson heard Abby's tone and became concerned.

"That clip you ran of Scarlett O'Hara's meltdown on British Airways," Charley said directly. "It's made our client very nervous. It needs to be taken off the website immediately, if not sooner."

Abby was taken aback. "You're asking me to kill a clip? Well, Charley, I can't do that."

"Please, Abby," Charley said, looking out to Vince at the pool. "I'm here to expedite whatever Vince Castle asks, and this was a direct order."

"Does he know that you and I know each other?"

"Not that I know of," Charley said. "But finding out who sent the video is the first thing he's asked me to do on this job, so it's important to me that I can get him the answer."

"I didn't know anyone still cared about Scarlett O'Hara," Abby said casually, glancing across the table.

At the mention of Scarlett's name, Jackson looked as if he'd been hit by lightning.

"Well, our client does since she's on the cover, so please do this for me?" Charley begged.

Abby couldn't take her eyes off Jackson. Even in the brisk winter afternoon he suddenly looked as if he was on fire. "I can take it down, but it's already gone viral. In other words, once it's out there, it's out there."

"Anything'll help," Charley said appreciatively. "And one more tiny—well, not so tiny—thing. My boss wants to fire whoever uploaded it to you."

Still staring at Jackson as he signaled the waiter for a second drink, Abby was calm with Charley. "I can't give up a source. You know that. Even for you."

"Can't you at least give me a hint? What kind of phone it came from…anything?" she pleaded. "I'll take it from there."

Abby breathed deeply. Charley was going to be her sister-in-law, after all.

"I got another clip from the same source an hour later. The second clip was at the Sandton Sun in Johannesburg, a shot of Oprah at a breakfast meeting," Abby told her. "In other words, it couldn't have been anyone who was traveling with you."

"Thanks, Abby," Charley sighed, relieved. "Thanks a zillion."

"You're welcome," Abby said quietly.

"Could I speak to Jackson for a second?" Charley asked.

"He's just taking a swig from a double tequila, but sure," Abby said dryly as she handed the phone to Jackson.

"Sis, hi," Jackson said, mustering a lilt in his voice. "So what's this about Scarlett?"

"She's one of the cover models, of all people," Charley said. "But this isn't about her. Did you or Chance tell Marlena and John that I was coming down here?"

"No. Chance and I were discussing just this morning how we haven't talked to them in a while, so I know he hasn't, either. And the not-so-obvious question is: why do you ask?"

"They're here."

"In South Africa?"

"I know. It's very weird. But coincidences happen, I guess. Like me being here with Scarlett."

"Yeah," Jackson said briskly.

"If you haven't seen that clip on Abby's website, you might want to see it. It happened after I told Scarlett you're engaged."

"Have a good time, Sis," was all Jackson could think of. "And get home soon." His voice held a hint of desperation.

"Thank Abby again," Charley said as she hung up the phone.

Jackson handed the phone back to Abby who just stared.

"Why did the name 'Scarlett O'Hara' turn you crimson?" Abby's heart was racing but she didn't know why.

Jackson took a deep breath. "She was my first."

"What?" Abby was thrown. "She's like twelve years older than you are."

Jackson met her gaze and shrugged. "I was seventeen, believe it or not, and we met at my birthday party at China White. She was a major model, and I guess I was fresh meat."

"The original cougar," Abby said dumbfounded. "Guess she belongs in Africa." She was trying to lighten the moment, but it didn't work. Jackson was still stone-faced.

"Then I have just one question," Abby said, gazing in his eyes. "Are you in love with her?"

"No…" Jackson insisted. But as Abby reached for his hand, he instead picked up his double tequila and finished it in one long gulp.

Please let that be the truth, she said to herself, feeling uneasy. Because you, Jackson Gaines, are supposed to be my future.

24 *CHARLEY, JOHN, AND MARLENA*

IT WAS FIVE ON THE DOT WHEN MARLENA AND JOHN WERE escorted to the reception lounge. They entered to find the entire photo crew in the far corner. The makeup, hair, and wardrobe people were at the ready as Vince took photo after photo, Charley near his side.

Scarlett was leaning against an opening that provided a view of the lush foliage outside and the soaring Drakensberg mountain range. A see-through African print tunic covered Scarlett's miniscule bikini top, and slim rust-colored leggings hugged her 35-inch inseam. Lounging on white cotton overstuffed chairs in the foreground were Brigitta and Nikki, dressed in ensembles that complemented what Scarlett was wearing. Red hair flowing over her shoulders, Scarlett was in profile, and from where John and Marlena stood, she was absolutely breathtaking.

"Yes...sultry...regal...good, very good...give me lioness," Vince directed as the girls shifted subtly. Their eyes, their postures, and their lips moved in ways that were nearly imperceptible to the naked eye but that were caught as dramatically different by

Vince's discerning lens. Vince checked the shots in his RZ67 as he went along, quickly deleting whichever didn't hit him instantly as brilliant.

"Look to me now…make love to the camera…make me want to eat you," he growled.

Checking the last shot, Vince scowled. "Greg, what's that under Red's left eye?" And before the makeup genius could answer, he added, "Fix it."

Greg moved in and dabbed at the corner of Scarlett's eye. "It's nothing, sugar," he assured her. "No biggie."

Scarlett touched the spot as Greg went back to Vince and whispered, "Crow's feet," under his breath.

"Crow's feet?" Vince said loudly enough for all to hear. Scarlett bit her lip as she saw Brigitta and Nikki exchange glances.

Brigitta hiccupped. "Don't worry, I only hiccup when I'm nervous…" she said.

"We're wrapped for now," Vince directed to the crew. "Everyone get set for tonight. We'll be shooting in the outside arena—"

"The 'boma'" Charley corrected him.

"Whatever," Vince said. "In the meantime, Charley's got your instructions."

Charley wasn't aware that she was in charge, but she had no problem picking up where he left off.

"Before anyone goes to rest up before getting back into hair and makeup, we're having a briefing by one of the rangers next door."

"With drinks?" Scarlett asked. The comment about her crow's feet hadn't helped the insecurity underneath her bravado.

"One, but no more," Vince barked before Charley could answer.

"The dinner's going to be amazing," Charley continued, ignoring Vince's interruption. "The chef here's earned three Michelin stars, and once we're sure we have the shots we want for the editorial, they will cater to your every whim. So if you see food that looks like crocodile, it just might be. But try it. I hear we'll all love it. By the way, has everyone taken their malaria pills today?"

Everyone chimed in that they had. Everyone except Scarlett.

"I—forgot mine," she lied.

"No, you dumped them in the toilet," Brigitta said innocently. "Remember?"

Scarlett glared at her newest competition.

"It's critical that everyone take them, even though I know it'll keep you from tanning, Scarlett," Charley said nicely. "They may have them here."

"Actually, we don't," Charley heard from behind her. It was the most beautiful voice she'd ever heard.

She turned to see the game ranger who was there for their briefing. She gasped. He was six feet tall with sandy floppy hair, dimples, and a cleft in his chin that she could get lost in.

"Brendan Fox," he said and smiled.

Are those teeth really yours? she wondered. Those eyes, those lips…

"Charley Gaines." She managed to smile back.

Am I drooling?

"We can get some tablets from one of the doctors in town if we need them," he said, smiling. Again.

From a few feet away Charley heard: "We can actually get them from the Tom-Ali Clinic if that would help."

Charley turned to see Marlena and John. She hadn't realized they'd been observing her.

"They're prescription," Brendan reminded her.

"I'm a psychiatrist," Marlena told him. "I can prescribe them for her, and I've volunteered there. I can make the call."

"Terrific, thanks." Brendan nodded. "If you guys want to coordinate it, that'll work."

He glanced at Charley, who smiled. Actually, she hadn't stopped smiling since she'd laid eyes on him.

∞

One of the requisites at any of the game farms was laying out the realities of being in the wilds of Africa. By the way Brendan comported himself while he gave the instructions, he obviously was very comfortable in his own skin.

"Londolani is one of the safest of the game farms in the Big Five area because we have two staff members for every guest. That means none of you ever have to worry about moving freely—as there'll always be someone to accompany you. As your personal guide told you when you arrived, it is imperative that you follow the rules. Because as supremely beautiful as it is here, it's dangerous. Last year, a pair of Asian tourists got out of their car to take photos of a lioness and her cubs, and were attacked and eaten."

Scarlett mimicked Asians taking photographs and snickered.

"It actually did happen, ma'am," Brendan said with a tone of admonishment.

Ma'am, Scarlett thought, grimacing to herself. Can't they at least call me Ms.?

"A few months ago, one tourist had her Shih Tzu with her, and when that puppy ran toward a herd of giraffe, she went after him. Got kicked by one of the giraffes and was dead instantly. It's no joke. Neither are the malaria tablets."

Scarlett shrank back in her seat. She didn't care how gorgeous Brendan was, she did not like to be criticized publicly.

"I understand I've only got two of this group going with me on the game ride this evening because the rest of you are working, but when you do go, you'll be in a six-passenger open Range Rover. There'll be a tracker in front with a rifle...we all carry guns, by the way...and it'll be his job to find the game if we need to. But we have every kind of species you'd expect to see here. Of course, the Big Five are—" He glanced to Charley.

"Buffalo, elephant, leopard, lion, and rhino," she stammered.

"Yep," he smiled back. "And we've got giraffe, wild dog, hyena, kudu, impala, cheetah, and hundreds of others. We'll point them out as we see them. And do *not* stand up in the vehicles. The animals have gotten to think of the Rovers as other creatures and recognize us by the silhouette. Standing up and waving your arms will just confuse them and they could attack. Truly.

"We don't want any fatalities, and not because we care about you. The animals will have tasted human blood and then have to be killed. Not cool. To us, they're as important as you are. Now, any questions?"

Scarlett's hand shot up. "I have one," she said with a sultry smile. "Where can we buy powdered rhino horn?"

Everyone froze as if they'd heard a gunshot.

"I'm sure I didn't hear you," Brendan finally said.

"Powdered rhino horn," Scarlett repeated. "Elle Macpherson said she took it, and she still looks amazing. Where can I buy it?"

"It's illegal," Charley snapped at her. "It's why rhino are being slaughtered for no good reason," she added passionately. "Do you ever read the news?"

Scarlett's back went up. "I read *USA Today*. Sometimes. Do I have to put up with this twit, Vince?" Scarlett snapped as she scanned the room for the director.

"I'm in charge at the moment, so yes, Scarlett, you do," Charley said, not backing down. "Now if Brendan is done, everyone can get ready for the next setup. Brendan, are you done?"

"I am now," he said, smiling. "And welcome to Africa, everyone."

The group dispersed. Some of the crew gave Charley a wink or a thumbs-up as they headed out, impressed with her fearlessness. Scarlett, however, ignored Charley as she passed her.

Charley took a deep breath. "I'm really sorry about her and for interrupting like that," she said to Brendan.

"You should have been a ranger," Brendan said with a smile, his deep brown eyes sparkling. "You know how to tame the wild ones."

Would that include you? she thought to herself.

"He's right. You were great, Charley," John said, suddenly beside her and pulling her out of her delicious thoughts.

"Thanks," was all she could say.

Brendan looked from John and Marlena back to Charley. "Are these your parents?" he asked.

Charley was thrown off guard. "Why would you think that?"

"You look like you could be related," he said warmly. "A compliment to you all, by the way, but sorry for that presumption."

"Thanks, and not a problem," John said, taking Marlena's hand.

"We actually are—related," Charley added. "It's a bit—complex."

"Okay," Brendan said, curious. But before they could go further, Brendan's tracker appeared in the open doorway.

"Mr. Brendan?" he signaled.

"We need to get out there if we're going to get back in time for dinner," Brendan offered.

"Maybe we'll see you then," John said to Charley.

"Maybe," she answered and glanced at Marlena. "Have a good time."

"I'll be there tonight, too," Brendan said as he smiled *that* smile at Charley.

She caught his gaze, returned the smile, and felt a rush of electricity from her toes to her brain.

Can he see my heart in my throat? She gulped.

He turned to John and Marlena. "Get ready for a life-changing few hours," he said as they headed out. "Another couple will be joining us. They're here several times a year and always take the first game ride they can. They're a great couple..."

Charley didn't move as she saw the three of them climb into the Range Rover where a well-heeled Asian couple waited. As the Rover headed into the lush vegetation, suddenly all Charley wanted was to be with the three of them, and that feeling startled her.

Why do I feel my life suddenly changing?

25  *PATCH AND KAYLA*

KAYLA WAS IN A PARTICULARLY GOOD MOOD WHEN SHE AND Steve returned home from the clinic. Not only had they provided much needed care to more than eighty people that day and a baby had been born, but she'd also seen one of her closest friends from home.

"Joe, Mommy and Daddy are home," she called out as she and Steve entered.

There was no answer.

"Yo, Joe Johnson, we're here," Steve reiterated.

Still, no answer.

"Hello? Violet?" Kayla said, puzzled as she moved through the living room while Steve headed toward the bedrooms.

"Joe?" Steve called with a bit of panic in his voice. Steve had worked as a private detective during one incarnation and was always acutely aware of any danger. Hoedspruit was generally safe for the white population, but in the last few years robberies at gunpoint had gotten more common.

"Hey!" Kayla heard in a loud enough whisper that she jumped.

It was Joe, sitting on a child's chair in the corner near the sliding door that opened to the deck.

He was in the naughty chair.

"Uh-oh," she said as she gave Joe a quizzical look. "Steve, he's out here."

"I didn't do anything," Joe insisted, defending himself although he hadn't been accused of anything.

Kayla knew her rambunctious son and wasn't so sure. "So Violet put you in the naughty chair because you were a good boy?"

"Yes," he smiled, his bright eyes crinkling.

Steve came from the hallway and saw Joe fidgeting and grinning. "And what did we do now, Sport?" he asked.

"Nothing," Joe said, wagging his head slowly from side to side.

"Where is Violet?" Kayla asked.

Joe pointed outside, and they could see her sweeping the deck as though she wanted to sweep it away, deck chairs and all.

Kayla opened the sliding door, and Violet looked up for the first time. Her face was solemn, and she was angry.

"Violet?" Kayla said as she joined her. "What happened?"

"He said he saw 'them,'" Violet said, her eyes blazing.

"Them?" Steve asked.

"Them." It was all Violet would say.

"The toggle-ishy!" Joe giggled as he jumped up from his seat.

"Stay!" Steve ordered as he pointed to Joe to sit down.

"Your papers were all over the floor, and he said 'they' threw them there," Violet said as she pointed inside the house. "He knows not to speak their name."

Striding past Kayla and Steve, Violet entered the house.

They had encountered things like this in the past, not with Violet but with their last housekeeper.

"The tokoloshi," Steve said quietly enough that Violet wouldn't hear.

"Their fables and mysteries are as real to them as the religions of some Anglos," Kayla said.

"Sure your leprechauns aren't as real as theirs?" Steve joked.

"Their gnarled little men are whirling devils to them, Steve," she said admonishingly. "And if anyone mentions they've seen one, that brings horrible luck. It's a curse."

That was true in some African cultures. They still held fast to their myths and mysticism and believed evil spirits existed. One of the most dangerous types of spirits, the tokoloshi, was released by even the mention of its name, and now Joe had done that in front of Violet.

Kayla and Steve could see the usually calm woman gathering her woven satchel and keys. Her hands were shaking badly.

"He needs to understand it's nothing to play with," Kayla said. "Where did he learn about that anyway?"

"I have no friggin' idea," Steve answered.

The tension was thick as the two entered the living room. Joe couldn't resist squealing, "Toggle-ishy!"

"Joe!" Kayla snapped. "Apologize to Violet right now, and never, ever, ever mention that name again, do you hear me?"

The two-and-a-half-year-old sat stock still and his lip started to quiver.

"I'm sorry..."

"Violet?" Kayla said imploringly.

"It's something bad, Miss Kayla, very bad," Violet said.

"Will you be back tomorrow?" Kayla asked. She knew this kind of thing could cripple those who believed in the spirits.

Violet looked around the room as if trying to sense its energy.

"No, Miss Kayla. No."

Steve and Kayla both knew it was hopeless to try and convince her.

"Let us pay you for this week at least," Steve offered. He knew the hardships those in her village endured.

"I'm sorry?" Joe repeated. Even at his young age he knew he was responsible for the tension swirling around them.

"I know," Violet answered gently.

Steve went to his desk, where his papers were now scattered on top, and took a metal box out of the drawer. He counted out three hundred rand, which amounted to less than forty dollars.

"Be safe," Violet told them as she headed out the door.

As she exited, Steve walked over and took Kayla in his arms.

"Maybe the bad luck we're getting from this whole tokoloshi thing is losing her," Steve offered, trying to comfort his wife.

"I hope so," Kayla said, trying to be optimistic. "It is so hard to find someone as capable as her. Maybe in time she'll come back."

"Can I get up now?" Joe asked as his parents still stared at the closed door.

"Come on, sweet boy," Kayla said, jolted back to reality. "Let's have some dinner and get you to bed."

"It was the toggle-ishy," Joe insisted.

"Joe!" Kayla admonished as she led him into the kitchen.

Steve put the metal box back in the drawer and began

straightening the disheveled papers. It had been a long day, and coming home to Joe acting up didn't make him happy. But he came across a beautiful photo Christmas card from their daughter, Stephanie, who was still back in Salem. She was in front of the family's Brady Pub, smiling from ear to ear.

It read, "Merry Christmas. I love you, Mom and Pops. When are you coming home?"

Steve's hand went to his chest. "I love you, too, baby, but we're here for a while longer."

Then he noticed, amid the pile, his and Kayla's bank statement. He opened it, and that smile from reading Stephanie's card vanished.

Kayla's last two salary checks bounced? he said to himself.

"Sweetie," he heard as Kayla came from the kitchen. "Dinner'll be in just a few."

He was jolted back to reality. "Thanks," he answered.

"Are you all right?" Kayla asked.

"Absolutely," he said as he slipped the letter into the drawer. "Just emotional over Steph's card."

Now I'm lying to my wife. Holy tokoloshi.

"But I'm not really hungry this early. You mind if I head over to Ambri for a quick one? They just reopened after the holiday…"

"You don't have to explain," Kayla answered. "See the guys, and I'll have Joe down by the time you get back. Then we can spend some together time."

Steve pulled her into his arms and gave her a tender kiss. "How do you get sweeter every day, Sweetness?" he asked, brushing her hair behind her ear.

"Knowing that you're always here to protect us makes every day better." She smiled with the smile that always melted his heart.

∞

Bill and Cornelius were at the bar when Patch entered. Ambri Africa's Bush Pub was one of their local hangouts. It bordered one of the game farms, so it was a great place to drink in the ambience of Africa. And it was a great place to drink, period.

"Hey," Patch said as he slid into a wooden chair next to Bill.

"Hey," Bill nodded.

"Can I get you a cold one?" Cornelius asked Patch as he stood. "Just going to get us another round."

"Sure," Patch answered with a sidelong glance at Bill.

"Two beers aren't going to send me over the edge," Bill said pointedly to him as Cornelius headed to the bar.

The atmosphere was lively, even early in the evening. With a pool table, a big-screen TV, and a pool outside on the deck, the pub was not only popular with the locals but also with the young international volunteers who worked at the camps. A smattering of dialects and languages flowed through the air.

"So, would you be comfortable approaching John Black?" Patch asked directly.

"About what?" Bill asked.

Patch rubbed his fingers and thumb together. "Cash."

Bill adamantly shook his head no. "We've got until the end of the month, and I've already got something in the works."

"The banks are not making loans, Bill," Patch reminded him.

"Kayla's last *two* checks bounced," Patch said flatly. "With me volunteering all my time down here, pretty soon we'll be in big trouble."

"What can I say?" Bill sighed.

"John's a good guy," Patch offered.

"Then get him to loan you some money," Bill said, ending the conversation abruptly as Cornelius returned with three iced pilsner glasses. "It is all going to work out. We have options." Raising his glass, he added, "To the future."

Cornelius raised his glass and the three men toasted.

Bill drank his long and slow. As he set the glass down, he frowned slightly and licked his lips several times.

"Are you sure this isn't a new brew?" he asked Cornelius.

"Carling Black Label," Cornelius assured him. "Same as always."

"My taster's off lately, I guess," Bill said shaking his head. "Anyone interested in a game?" he asked, pointing to the pool table and changing the subject.

"One and then I have to head over to Londolani," Cornelius said. "Have to pick up some malaria tablets and take them to a supermodel, I hear."

"Tough job, but someone's got to do it," Bill joked. As they stood, he stumbled and had to catch his footing. He didn't notice as Cornelius and Patch exchanged concerned glances.

"Later," Patch simply said.

"Later," Bill answered and headed to play.

Patch watched as Cornelius greeted a few of the locals while Bill racked the billiard balls on the table. When Patch stepped outside the pub, the sun was setting over the Timbavati, and white rhinos and elephants were emerging for their nightly dinner. The darkening sky was aflutter as white-backed vultures circled in the distance, indicating a kill.

26  SCARLETT

SCARLETT WAS NOT HAPPY WHEN SHE RETURNED TO HER suite with Brigitta and Nikki.

Though the accommodations were absolutely gorgeous, Scarlett did not like the idea of sharing with two younger models. The fact that the central living area was being used for wardrobe, hair, and makeup didn't help. Even though the suite was massive and the rooms luxurious and totally private, she did not like it.

"There have to be other rooms," she snapped to their Xsoha attendant.

"I understand we are full, ma'am," he said, smiling graciously. "Perhaps if you spoke to your girl in charge, she could arrange something."

"Who's that? Charley?" She scoffed and rolled her eyes. "Let her sleep in here, and I'll sleep with Vince? Yeah, that's going to happen."

Nikki and Brigitta exchanged glances.

"Is there anything I could get for you, ma'am?" he asked pleasantly.

"Ma'am? Arsenic, maybe," she said dryly.

"I don't believe we have any, ma'am," he answered, not realizing she was just being her snide self.

As Scarlett glared at him, Nikki and Brigitta stifled amused laughter.

"Ashley and the gang'll be here in an hour," Nikki offered. "I'm going to catch a few winks until then. And thank you, Uuka, for everything," she added graciously to the attendant. "We appreciate it."

He nodded pleasantly and exited.

Nikki was beautiful, in her late twenties, and the most accommodating model any of the top photographers worked with. In the biz, she was considered a gem, and she worked constantly, to Scarlett's chagrin.

"I am definitely talking to my agent about this when I get back," Scarlett spat. "And you should, too," she told the girls as they went into their room. "I'm just looking out for all of us!"

As they disappeared, Scarlett could hear Brigitta ask, "Are Charley and Vince Castle sleeping together?"

"If they are, it's none of our business," Nikki could be heard replying faintly. "But don't listen to anything Scarlett says...you know her reputation."

The door closed behind them as Scarlett bristled. "My reputation?"

With the other girls gone, the room felt even more enormous. By herself now, Scarlett wrapped her arms around her torso and her bravado faded. As she turned, she caught sight of her image in one of the full-length mirrors.

Turning to the side, Scarlett cupped her breasts in her hands over her clothes and lifted them. When she released them, her breasts dropped to their natural position. She frowned. She then turned to check her tush and tightened her glutes. As soon as she released them, her butt dropped more than she'd expected.

Slowly, she moved close to the mirror and her hand went to her left eye.

Crow's feet? she thought to herself. What next, a turkey neck? I might as well be a bird.

The sounds of birds fluttering caught her attention. She watched as white-backed vultures soared in the distance. The sky was a deep turquoise now, with the setting sun casting a coral glow over the landscape. She stood mesmerized as the birds began circling not far from the camp.

After a few moments, she went into her room, closed her door, and shrugged out of the elegant African-print sportswear she'd worn for the first photo setup.

Naked, she lay on the massive white duvet that covered her king-sized bed. Her cell phone was on the side table. She studied it for what seemed an eternity and then reached for it.

As she started to dial, she realized it read, "No Service."

She put down the phone and ran her hand across the big, empty bed. Then she noticed a landline on the other side table.

Gathering courage, she dialed for an outside line and gave the operator a number she knew by heart. The number rang several times before she heard: "Jackson Gaines…"

"Jackson, it's your blast from the—"

"…I'm not able to take your call, so leave a name and number at the tone, and I'll return your call as quickly as possible…" the voice interrupted.

Voicemail, she realized.

Then there was that all-too-familiar beep.

Flustered, Scarlett said "Hey, lover, when you get a chance, call me. I ran into that squirt of a sister of yours, and you probably know that, but, well, hi—and bye."

Scarlett hung up and grimaced.

"Why did I ever let you go?" she said softly.

27  CORNELIUS

SEVERAL BLACK BUTTON SPIDERS SCURRIED ALONG THE wall of the Tom-Ali Clinic as Cornelius clicked on the lights. Known as black widows in the United States, the spiders lived up to their namesake's reputation: they were beautiful but dangerous.

Cornelius was used to them coming from the cracks that had appeared in the walls over the last few years, so he paid no attention as he moved to the locked, wall-sized medicine cabinet.

Inside were rows and rows of various medications, most donated by the government, sponsored charitable organizations, or pharmaceutical companies.

He took bottles of the three antimalaria meds for Scarlett and put them in his duffel. As he was closing the cabinet, he stopped and perused the wealth of pharmacology at his disposal.

After a long moment, he reached for a bottle of Rohypnol.

"Roofies," he said wryly to himself as he slipped it in with the other bottles. The drug was so versatile that it could be used as a sedative, an animal tranquilizer, or an amnesiac agent.

He locked the cabinet and smiled. Then he moved to a mirror

that hung on the far wall and checked his image. He adjusted his collar, slicked back loose hair behind his ears, and grinned.

Heading out of the clinic, he turned off the lights and locked the door behind him.

The night was gorgeous, hot and steamy, with the stars shining brighter than he'd ever remembered.

Climbing into the Tom-Ali van, he clicked on his radio and South African jazz megastar Andre Schwartz's music filled the air.

After checking to make sure his rifle was secure on the seat next to him, Cornelius headed down the gravel road to the Royal Londolani to bring the meds to Scarlett. By now the animals were emerging, escaping the heat of the summer day.

Sleek zebra.

Graceful giraffe.

And the predatory jackal.

28  MARLENA AND JOHN

THE WARM GLOW OF TORCHES LIT THE PATH TO THE RECEP-
tion lodge as Brendan drove the Rover back from the game ride.
While the lush summer foliage often made viewing animals more
difficult, their ride had been incredibly rewarding. Aside from the
kudu, impala, and giraffe they'd spotted, they had come upon two
lionesses in the same pride with cubs less than two months old.
Brendan had stopped the Rover for nearly forty minutes, quietly
observing as the cubs suckled; their mothers groomed them; and
they tussled with each other playfully as they found their footing.

"That was absolutely phenomenal," Marlena said to Brendan as
they all climbed out of the open truck.

"We were so lucky," her Asian counterpart said. "Seeing
moments like those is one of the reasons we come back here so
often." Jiao-jie and her husband, Wen, were frequent visitors to
Londolani. In their mid-thirties, they had the carriage and sophistication that spoke of Chinese royalty, and Wen's surname, Xing,
gave every indication that they were.

"How many trips have you made here?" John asked Wen casually.

"Ten perhaps?" Wen asked his wife.

"At least." She smiled warmly. "There is no better place to escape the chaos of Hong Kong than here."

"And you?" Wen asked John.

"First time for me," John responded. "But Doc was in the area years ago when she volunteered at one of the clinics in Hoedspruit."

"A doctor!" Jiao-jie said, impressed. "I wanted to study medicine, but my father insisted on law. Not exactly the same personal satisfaction as being a surgeon."

"I'm actually a psychiatrist," Marlena offered.

"But you help people nonetheless," Jiao-jie said.

"So do we," Wen interrupted.

"How?" his wife asked.

"By providing them with things to cure their itch to spend money," he joked. His smile was engaging.

"We're importers," Jiao-jie admitted. "Londolani is one of the stops we make all over Africa."

"Lucky you," John remarked.

"In fact, you'll find a few of their trinkets in our gift shop," Brendan added. "And in the photo shoot."

"Expensive trinkets, I suspect," John said.

"Only the best for your wife—and mine," Wen said, smiling.

"It's pretty amazing stuff," Brendan said. "The shop's open after the morning ride, and you should take a look. But now it's time for dinner."

Brendan nodded to two staff members who were at the ready.

"After those delicious sundowners, I'm not sure I'm hungry," Jiao-jie said. Sundowners were the champagne and delicate appetizers that were served under the stars halfway through every evening ride. Local fruits, grilled vegetables and rich cheeses, caviar on toast points, and indeterminate but delicious grilled meat on skewers had been on the ride's menu.

"Could we not discuss the sundowners?" Marlena grimaced, embarrassed.

"Whatever you want, Doc," John said as he bit his lip to keep from laughing. "But it was an experience to remember."

Marlena punched him lightly as the three others managed to stifle their laughter.

"If you'd like to freshen up first," Brendan told Marlena, "we can meet in the boma in thirty minutes. The photo shoot should be done by then."

∞

The photo shoot was indeed close to wrapping when Brendan escorted Marlena and John into the enclosure at the far end of the camp. The "boma" was lit with torches, sending golden light flickering off the woven, thorny brush that created the high walls of the hidden fortress. Scarlett, Brigitta, and Nikki wore brightly colored simple summer sheaths accented with handcrafted big, bold African jewelry as they danced with staff members in traditional garb.

"Scarlett, I need more in your eyes…Scarlett! Give me sex…let's see it…Brigitta, raise those arms high…Nikki, yes, powerful, but give me more…Come on, girls," Vince commanded as he moved from girl to girl taking shots of them gyrating wildly while a tribal band played ngoma drums and musical bows.

"Don't stop!" he added as he moved to look through the shots. From Vince's expression, Charley could see he wasn't totally pleased. "Scarlett, Nikki—switch places," Vince heard from behind as an amped Charley directed the models effortlessly.

"What?" Scarlett scoffed.

"What are you doi—?" Vince said as he whirled to see Nikki glide into Scarlett's circle, while Charley led the reluctant Scarlett into Nikki's place.

The resulting image was spot-on. The orange of Nikki's dress mirrored the paint that streaked the face of one of the young dancers, while Scarlett's deep rose was the color of the bangles up the leg of another.

"Brilliant," Vince shouted. "Great eye, girl, great eye…"

After several more shots of the dizzyingly sensual scene, Vince pumped his fist in the air repeatedly. "That's—a—wrap—fabulous!"

Nikki and Brigitta were exhausted but exuberant. Scarlett's expression was less than enthusiastic. The deep thumping of the drums and the gongs, rattles, and strings crescendoed as the powerful noise ended with a bang.

"Makeup call time is 3:00 a.m.," Charley chimed in as the group dispersed.

The dancers bowed to each other, while the musicians sat stock-still. John wolf-whistled and Marlena applauded loudly.

Charley whirled to see them there again. Just then, Vince patted her on the back and repeated, "Great eye, girl, great eye. Must've gotten it from your mother."

Brendan couldn't help but notice John and Marlena exchanging glances.

"There's a light dinner set up for you all in the suite. Get to sleep *early*," Vince demanded.

"Call time 3:00 a.m., we know, we know!" Scarlett spluttered as she slid past Charley. Everyone from hair, makeup, and wardrobe followed.

John and Marlena parted to let them pass. As Scarlett moved through, she caught her first real sight of John. Dashing. Handsome, she thought. Just plain hot.

Caught off guard, Scarlet tripped in her Christian Louboutin heels and awkwardly tumbled forward.

John, being John, swept her up before she hit the ground.

"You've got a lot of work to do, darlin'," he said, smiling. "Wouldn't want any bruises on that beautiful face."

Scarlett melted.

"Right, Doc?" John said as he glanced to his wife.

But Marlena was totally unaware of the interchange. Her focus was on Charley, who was now in deep conversation with Vince as they clicked through the shots taken earlier.

"Be careful," John told Scarlett. "We want this shoot to be perfect."

Before Scarlett could ask why it would matter to John, Brigitta started hiccupping. Again.

"Excuse us?" Nikki said, smiling, as John righted Scarlett. "And sorry if we've interrupted your vacation."

"We knew there was a photo shoot here when we booked," John said. "It was all last minute, and they were totally up front, so not a problem. Besides, this is all pretty intriguing."

"Very," Scarlett said as she attempted to lock eyes with John.

But he was now fixated on Marlena who was fixated on Vince still in deep, close conversation with their daughter.

"Uuka can walk you back," Brendan said to the models.

Uuka was just outside the entrance and indicated for them to lead the way.

"Doc?" John said to Marlena as soon as the girls and the other talent had exited. "You okay?"

"Just being me," she said, giving him a look and glancing back at Vince and Charley. "I know…the overprotective mother."

Brendan's tanned brow furrowed as he overheard the comment.

Marlena noticed his reaction and sighed. "As Charley said, it's all a bit complex."

29  *CORNELIUS*

A LIGHT WIND WAS BLOWING AS CORNELIUS WALKED THE elevated path to one of the magnificent Londolani suites. In the distance he could hear the sounds of the tribal band from the boma. The rhythms were dynamic, frenzied, and highly sexual.

He smiled to himself. *All this and supermodels, too. One dumb enough to throw away her malaria tablets.*

There was a rustle of leaves in the nearby bushes. Cornelius stayed on the path but moved to the edge. He could see several small wild cats scurrying through the brush.

As the music ended, he heard a wolf whistle and some applause followed by some muffled chatter. Then there were footsteps behind him.

Cornelius turned to see Wen and Jiao-jie being escorted toward the boma by a tall African who carried a wooden jewelry case.

"Mr. and Mrs. Xing," Cornelius said. "Good to see you."

"Very nice to see you, too." Jiao-jie smiled. "How has everything been at the clinic since we last saw you?"

"Couldn't be better," Cornelius stated. "Is that your newest collection?" he asked as he indicated the box in the African's hand.

"Exquisite platinum pieces with blue diamonds," Jiao-jie said. "We're dropping them with the concierge and then heading to dinner. Will we see you while we're here?"

"If you have the time, yes," he answered.

"We never did thank you properly for your fine work," Wen said. "Look, barely a scar."

Wen held out his hand and Cornelius inspected it. On one of the Xings' trips, Wen had sliced his hand badly and Cornelius had been called to the game farm to stitch the wound. The scar that ran across Wen's palm was barely visible.

"If I ever need plastic surgery, I know who to call," Jiao-jie teased.

"Speaking of plastic surgery," Wen said as he nodded toward the boma. Scarlett, Nikki, and Brigitta were headed toward them, followed by makeup, hair, the stylist, and Uuka, of course. "You can't tell me they haven't had it."

"Those perfect bodies are totally natural, darling." Jiao-jie smiled. "Or not."

"Excuse me," Scarlett sniped as they walked up, "but this is our suite."

"And lovely to meet you, too, miss." Jiao-jie smiled as she bowed her head slightly.

"Well, thank you," Scarlett said, startled.

"Miss?" she thought. *Finally!*

"If you'll excuse us now," Jiao-jie said. "So nice running into you again, Cornelius."

"Same back," he answered.

Wen and Jiao-jie headed toward the game lodge as the girls entered their suite, the entourage behind them.

∽

The girls began undressing immediately, slipping off their two-thousand-dollar shoes and jewelry, and shrugging out of their clothes.

Accustomed to stripping down after a shoot, it took a few minutes before Nikki noticed that Cornelius had entered and was watching transfixed as they disrobed.

"Can we help you?" she asked simply. Even the slightest movement of her face lit it up like sunrise on the Kalahari.

"I don't suppose you're—Scarlett O'Hara." He smiled as he checked the prescription labels on the malaria tablets.

"Do I look like a Scarlett O'Hara?" Nikki chuckled.

"More like Halle Berry," he said, smiling as he moved closer. "But you've probably been told that a thousand times."

"One or two," she replied with a smile.

Cornelius could barely rip his gaze away from Nikki. Her smile was engaging and her full, coral-painted lips inviting.

"Yoo-hoo," Scarlett said as she waved her nearly forty-year-old arms. "Those for me?"

"If you're the one who tossed her malaria tablets, yes they are," Cornelius said, turning to face her.

"That's moi," Scarlett admitted as she glared at Brigitta.

"I'm also supposed to make sure you take them," Cornelius said as he handed them over. "It is important, Scarlett. It's like shingles. If you get malaria, it'll haunt you for the rest of your life." The half-nude models around him might have distracted Cornelius, but he knew his job.

"Here's some water," Brigitta chirped as she grabbed a bottle of mineral water.

"Thanks a heap." Scarlett smiled weakly. She opened the bottle, dumped the tablets in her hand, and then downed the bitter pills. Her face screwed up as if she'd eaten cat food. "I'd rather take powdered rhino horn," she said as she shuddered. "Couldn't taste any worse than this!"

Cornelius reeled. "Rhino horn?"

Nikki shook her beautiful head at Scarlett, disgusted. "Don't listen to her. We know it's illegal...and inhumane."

"Just kidding," Scarlett threw back at them. But they all knew she'd pay a fortune if she could get her acrylic nails around some.

"Rhino poaching's increased two thousand percent in the last year," Cornelius snapped. He was angry, and the veins on his neck showed it.

"Sorr-y" Scarlett said as she tossed her bright red curls.

"This isn't funny," Cornelius added. "It's an epidemic, Scarlett...no, it's a tragedy, and even joking about it is pathetic."

The room was quiet as everyone just stared.

"Okay, okay, I am sorry," Scarlett said in as apologetic a tone as she could. "Really. I just thought if it's true that Elle Macpherson uses—"

"Shut your pie hole, Scarlett!" Nikki said.

"Whoa," Scarlett said, backing up. "Yes, ma'am."

"Okay..." Nikki trailed off. Then she looked at Cornelius. "And while you are absolutely adorable, and I not only love your passion about this and appreciate the way you look at me, I'm a married woman—"

"—Cornelius," he said.

"Cornelius," she completed.

"And her husband is a defensive tackle for the Green Bay Packers," Brigitta added. "Big guy. Huge."

"I also have a gorgeous son and a precious daughter, both under five, who I adore. So if you're looking for more than a drop-off on those meds tonight, I'm not the place to look," Nikki added.

"Did I put out that vibe?" Cornelius asked. He'd been put in his place and he knew it.

"Kind of," Brigitta said, nodding.

"I am sorry about all that," Cornelius said to Nikki. "But your husband's one lucky guy. You are a gorgeous woman."

Ashley, the usually quiet stylist, stepped in. "Come on, guys, it was a long flight, a long day, and we've got a—"

"Three a.m. call," everyone said simultaneously.

"Then my apologies to you all, truly," Cornelius stated. "I know you're here to work, and I actually have an early call tomorrow, too. So…"

"Good night?" Nikki said.

"Good night," Cornelius answered. "And make sure she takes those things every day, Nikki," he said, indicating Scarlett.

"'Night," Scarlett seethed.

"Ta," Brigitta said with a hiccup. "Oh!"

There was a moment of silence after Cornelius exited; the only sounds were those from nature that lurked right outside their suite.

"Let's finish up, guys," Ashley said.

They all went back to prepping for the morning as Scarlett stared at the closed door.

Make sure "she" takes the pills? Scarlett said to herself. What am I, chopped liver?

30 VINCE, CHARLEY, AND BRENDAN

BRENDAN COULD SENSE THE UNDERCURRENT BETWEEN Vince and Charley.

Charley was, after all, one of those girls who had "it." At least the "it" Brendan was looking for. And if anyone had asked her, she'd have said the same about him.

The problem was that he could tell Vince had "it," too. Vince had gone through the requisite party scenes in New York, London, and the South of France and had developed a reputation as not only a celeb photographer but also a confirmed womanizer. His reputation was as huge as his god-given "gifts."

When he set his well-trained eye on a woman, she was helpless. And Vince had not often come across a female as desirable and unobtainable as Charley Gaines. Brendan had seen the way Vince looked at Charley during the shoot in the boma. It was a look indicating an interest in being more than just boss and assistant. It was the look of a predator with his prey. And since Brendan's job was to protect his guests from the predators, he decided to offer to be their escort back to the suite.

When Brendan approached Charley and Vince and told them he'd be escorting them, Charley's heart leapt into her throat. I'm not drooling, she said to herself as she wiped her mouth. But can he hear my heart beating?

Charley's heart rate was so strong that she could have sworn the ngoma drums were still pounding. She also knew she had a stupid grin on her face, but she hoped the low light of the glowing torches kept Brendan from seeing it.

"Thanks," Vince said. "But we know where we're headed."

"And I'd lose my job if I let you go alone, Mr. Castle," Brendan answered. "You never know what dangers are lurking in the shadows around here."

His steady gaze met Vince's.

"If I didn't know better, I'd think you're trying to tell me something," Vince shot back with a sly grin.

"We should get a move on, unless you're staying for dinner," Brendan answered. He was trying to be neither confrontational nor snarky. Whatever he felt about Vince Castle at the moment, he was still a paying guest at Londolani. "Not sure you realized the other guests are already here."

Brendan indicated John and Marlena, now conversing with Wen and Jiao-jie who'd just arrived.

"Then let's hit it," Vince said, smiling.

Charley led the way, which brought her face to face with John and Marlena.

"This was all really fascinating, Charley," Marlena said, smiling.

"Thank you," Charley answered.

Why do I have to deal with this now? Charley thought.

"John Black," John said, extending his hand to Vince. "Sorry if we're at all in the way here."

"I didn't expect other people here during the shoot, but I guess everyone has to make money. Even the people who have it," Vince answered as he ignored John's gesture. "If you'll excuse us, we still have a lot to do."

Vince indicated for Charley to move on.

"Maybe we can link up tomorrow," she said to John, though her voice held little conviction.

"We'll see," John answered. He was smart enough not to push. "Have a good night."

"You, too," Charley answered before nodding to Marlena.

The moment was awkward as Marlena merely nodded in return. Charley was very aware that Brendan had witnessed it all.

∞

"I hear you're shooting at the watering hole tomorrow morning," Brendan said, making conversation as they headed to the suite.

"We are," Charley answered. "Will you be there?"

The minute that came out of her mouth, Charley regretted it. I sound like I'm twelve, she thought.

"Tomorrow's my day off." Brendan smiled. "But I'm sure you'll have a terrific experience. It's the best place for spotting all kinds of wild creatures."

"Guess that's why we're shooting there," Vince said, shaking his head. "And here we are, my friend, so thanks again."

Vince opened the handcrafted door and indicated for Charley to go in first.

"I'll be right there," she said, which surprised even her.

"Well, fine," Vince answered. "But we've got a lot of prep for tomorrow."

Charley nodded and Vince reluctantly went inside. She and Brendan were alone for the first time, and now she was flustered.

"Well, thanks for walking us back," she said.

"My pleasure," he answered. "I was impressed with how you handled everyone tonight. We all were."

"Yes...all," she said. "That's what I wanted to talk to you about. I know you can see there's something going on between me and John and Marlena Black."

"Yep," was his simple answer. "But I also know it's none of my business."

But it is your business, she thought, gazing into his eyes. I'm not sure why yet, but it is.

"I lost both of my parents last year..." she said, her voice trailing off.

"And they stepped in," Brendan answered for her.

"It's not quite that simple," Charley said.

"Well, for what it's worth, I like them," Brendan said. "Especially after what happened on the ride."

Charley gave him a quizzical look.

"I don't usually show anyone videos I've taken of other guests, but..." he said.

Charley was more curious than ever.

"We tell everyone to be careful when they have to 'go,' because this is Africa and there are no porta-potties in the wild. We'd finished our sundowners, and Marlena needed to 'freshen up,' so she did." He smirked. "When she was done, I caught this on my iPhone."

Brendan pulled out the iPhone and opened a video taken at the end of their stop for sundowners under a sprawling Umbrella Thorn tree.

Charley watched and her eyes widened.

There in living color was Marlena, walking calmly from a large thicket of bushes and totally unaware of the toilet paper streaming out of the back of her pants and the three massive rhinos trailing her.

"Oh, no…!" Charley couldn't help but laugh.

"She was a real trouper, though," Brendan said. "I got everyone back into the Rover with no problem, but that was one dangerous little moment."

"Really?" Charley asked, not believing it.

"Worst-case scenario, she actually could have been attacked, maybe killed."

The words cut through Charley like a knife.

"But she was fine, so apologetic and really down to earth about it. Won over my heart actually. She has a great story to tell, and so do I in my next briefing."

"Wow," Charley said softly.

"Charley!" they heard from inside.

"I've got to go in," Charley said, her mind still reeling. "I guess I won't see you tomorrow."

"I should be around in the evening," Brendan answered pointedly. "You be careful," he added as he indicated Vince.

Charley realized Brendan was being protective, and she liked it.

"His bark is worse than his bite," she answered.

"It had better be," he said, flashing that drool-inducing smile she found irresistible. "We all carry handguns and have rifles in our Rovers, remember?"

31   *PATCH AND KAYLA*

Kayla was sitting at Steve's desk going through her phone book when he finally returned home. She was so intent on what she was doing that she didn't hear him enter.

So when he put a bouquet of hot orange and pink daisies with coral summer roses under her nose, she nearly jumped out of her skin.

"Steve!" she gasped.

"Sorry, Sweetness, it's just little ol' me," Steve said gently.

Kayla took a deep breath and leaned back in the chair.

"I'm the one who's sorry," she said. "And those are absolutely beautiful, thank you."

"Grown just for you." He kissed her fully on the mouth and then grinned.

Steve's grin had always gotten her, from the time she'd laid eyes on him more than twenty years earlier. He had that crooked, bad-boy smile that more often than not led to seduction. And the roses were indeed from the summer garden Steve had planted when they'd arrived in Hoedspruit a little more than two years earlier. Little did his friends from home realize that Steven "Patch" Johnson now loved getting his hands in the dirt.

"Let me put them in water," Kayla said, touching his cheek.

Steve watched as she set her phone book next to the pile of mail he'd gone through earlier. The mail that included the bank statement he hoped she hadn't seen.

As Kayla rose from the desk, she caught a glimpse of Steve's clouded expression.

"Honey, is something going on?" she asked.

Steve hesitated for a nanosecond. Where did loyalty lie? With Bill, who he'd promised to keep the news of their decaying funds from everyone for now, or with his wife, whose passion was on the line?

"Nothing. Just thinking about how Joe's getting to be a handful," was his answer.

Was skirting the truth a lie?

"He is." Kayla sighed with a hint of concern. "When I put him down, he still insisted it was the tokoloshi."

"Kids and their imaginary friends," Steve answered. "Who knows? Maybe he'll be a great writer someday."

Kayla couldn't be as glib.

"Maybe it's better that Violet is gone. As much as I love her, she's so superstitious, and maybe that wasn't good for Joe."

"True, but who do we get to replace her?" Steve asked.

"So many people here need work that we'll find someone. I hope. But I just went through my entire phone book and came up empty."

"You said Beauty's always been great with the kids at the clinic," Steve reminded her.

Kayla let it sink in. Beauty could be a great choice.

"She's in tomorrow. I'll talk to her and see, but I'm not sure taking care of one small tornado of a boy is going to thrill her. I wonder what Bill pays her," Kayla said.

I wonder *if* he pays her, Steve thought.

"In the meantime, can you watch him tomorrow, Steve?" She went on before he could answer. "If not, I'll have to bring him with Marlena and me to the weavers."

"We'll work it out, Sweetness," Steve answered. "We always do."

"True," she said, smiling softly. "We always do.

She moved across the polished wood floors to a cabinet above the sink. As she reached up to take out a heavy South African cut-glass vase, she winced, her hand going to her neck.

Steve watched as she filled the vase with water and arranged the freshly cut flowers and greens with the simple artistry of a florist.

"Beautiful," Kayla said as she set the vase on the dining-room table and bent to catch a whiff of the fragrant roses. Her hand again went to her neck.

Before she could remove it, Steve's hand was on hers. He moved it gently, massaging the aching area with his masculine fingers.

"Can you work it out?" Kayla said softly of the ache in her neck.

"I always do," he repeated softly.

The very feel of his flesh against hers calmed her, and she began to relax immediately. His warm lips against her neck caused her to shudder.

"Much better…" Kayla purred and easily moved her head from side to side. Then she turned to face Steve and rose on her toes to kiss him deeply.

Steve responded, and their lips and tongues explored each other's with a mixture of passion and purity.

There were no sounds except the rustling of nature and the quickening of their breath as Steve lifted her onto the dining table. Kayla wrapped her bare legs around the back of his thighs and pulled closer.

"How soundly is Joe sleeping?" Steve asked in what was almost a moan.

"Soundly enough to not hear us through two closed bedroom doors," Kayla whispered.

Steve untied the belt from her cotton wrap dress and slipped his hands behind her. As he hoisted her up in his arms, Kayla wrapped her legs around his hips and her arms around his shoulders.

Steve lifted her from the table as if she was a feather and danced with her gently as he carried her to the bedroom. It was as if they could feel each other pulsing, the tempos matching as they glided across the room.

Above the soft chirping of the crickets they could hear the soft mating calls of the African gray parrots in the distance. Steve and Kayla, however, had already found their mates.

32  MARLENA AND JOHN

MARLENA WAS SITTING ON THE EDGE OF THEIR PRIVATE rim-flow pool, her legs dangling in the cool water as she stared out into the night.

It was pitch black, which meant the bushveld was teeming with life through the dense foliage. The croaking of African frogs, the chirping of crickets, and a variety of unfamiliar animal sounds were complemented by the slight splashing sounds in the water.

Part of John's rehabilitation was swimming, and he took every opportunity to enjoy it. Especially in the dense warmth of the African summer night at the feet of the woman he adored.

The gentle lapping of the water stopped as John's face emerged from the water in front of Marlena. He slid up her well-toned calves to rest his head on her knees.

His hands slid along her bare thighs, and he cupped her hips in his strong but gentle hands. The touch of her skin excited him and she welcomed him, but he could sense some distance.

"It's going to be all right, Doc," John said as he looked up at her.

"Is it?" she asked.

"Are you sorry we came?" he answered.

"No…" she insisted. "Well, maybe a bit. But only because of Charley. Guess I didn't need to say that, did I?" she added rhetorically.

"We had no way of knowing she'd be here," John said. "And I don't think we need to avoid her. We're all adults."

"She's nineteen and obviously conflicted," Marlena said. "And we aren't her parents except for the biology of it, anyway. If Olivia and Ritchie were both still alive, it would probably be very, very different. But I feel responsible for her."

"So do I," John admitted. "But if she wants us in her life, we will be, and if she doesn't, we'll have to live with it. We've got one great set of kids as it is, you know."

"I know." Marlena smiled softly.

"You're prettier when you smile, you know," he said, cocking his eyebrow

"Everyone is," Marlena answered, deflecting John's attempt to connect with her.

"I'm pretty proud of whatever we offered genetically to that child, by the way," John said. "She does have your smiling eyes."

"She is amazing," Marlena admitted. "And here we are in this glorious, still night, with nothing but the moon, the stars, and whatever's feasting on the trees ten feet away, and I have the most wonderful man in the world naked in front of me, wanting me, and all I can think about is her."

"I get that," John smiled ruefully. "Maybe if you joined me in the water, it could help you focus on other things. Just for tonight."

Marlena's gaze met his. She adored this man, and she wanted to please him. She slipped her arms out of the short, light robe she wore and put her hands on John's shoulders as he slowly slid her toward him and into the water.

The water was cooler than Marlena had imagined, but it heated up quickly between them as John drew her to him.

Her breasts pressed against his strong chest, and her arms slipped around his waist.

The water, so still, began lapping gently around them as they began to move in rhythm. With the buoyancy of the water, they moved effortlessly, weightlessly. Their water ballet began lyrically and slow, and then built. As Marlena melted into her lover's embrace, the "prrrps" and loud hoots of the owls in nearby trees startled them. And made them laugh.

"Exhibitionist," John teasingly scolded his wife.

"At least they liked it," she said smiling widely. "And I know I'm prettier when I smile."

"Let's try to keep it then, Doc." John smiled back warmly. "Now can we get out of here? Believe it or not, I'm getting cold."

∽

After a warm shower together, John and Marlena climbed between the crisp white sheets on the four-poster bed and lowered the mosquito netting.

Marlena snuggled into John's flesh, and he wrapped his arms around her.

"Better?" John asked.

"Better," Marlena answered.

"'Night," John said.

"'Night," she responded simply.

Neither could see that the other was still wide awake. John was concerned about his beautiful wife, and she was concerned about their daughter.

33  *CHARLEY*

CHARLEY LAID HER HEAD ON THE CUSHY DOWN PILLOW, the digital clock by her bed flipped to read twelve straight up. Midnight. It had been an astonishing forty-eight hours since the midnight that had started this whole adventure. Had she left Jackson and Chance at the Trafalgar Hotel even moments before on New Year's Eve, Vince may not have found her and she wouldn't have been offered the job that brought her here.

She yawned widely, stretching out on the bed. It was rumored that almost everyone who was anyone had stayed at the Royal Londolani—from Justin Timberlake and Elton John to Julia Roberts and honeymooning Chelsea Clinton and hubby Marc Mezvinsky—but the rumors had never been confirmed. The Royal Londolani was discreet to the max.

Still, as she tried to sleep, Charley mulled over the fact that she could be sleeping in the same bed where entertainment royalty and true royalty had slept. It never occurred to Charley that, to some, she was actually royalty.

She wished it wasn't so late. Call time was in less than three hours. If anyone knew that, she did. But she and Vince had had plenty to do once they got back to their suite. They had gone through all of the photos from the day, but unfortunately, not many were good. The truth was that Scarlett's shots weren't cutting it, and Vince was getting uncharacteristically nervous.

He'd had two hits of weed to try to calm his nerves and had offered some to her, but Charley wasn't interested. She didn't have an issue with smoking pot; it just wasn't her thing. She also wanted to make sure the boundaries were drawn with Vince Castle. Vince's reputation was legendary. Brendan was right to be protective, she thought.

Brendan. She couldn't resist smiling as she said his name.

Brendan Fox. Charley and Brendan. Charley Fox.

She sat bolt upright.

I didn't really think that, did I?

Though she was alone, she was mortified. Well, maybe just a little mortified, she thought. I guess it's true: a girl meets a guy she thinks is hot, and before you can say "I do," she's trying out their names together.

Charley sank back into her pillow and let the name roll around in her mind: Charlotte "Charley" Fox. And he likes John and Marlena, she thought to herself.

As she turned to adjust her position on the comfy mattress, Charley caught sight of something on the bedside table. It was the family album Marlena had so meticulously put together.

Time was slipping by quickly, and Charley had less than three hours to sleep. But the book was there, staring at her. She closed her eyes, but it was hopeless. She was alone in this very safe zone, and there was no way she could get her new life out of her mind. So she gathered the book and took it back to bed with her.

For the first time, she opened the pages. As she flipped through, they told the intriguing, romantic, dangerous, heartbreaking, and triumphant story of John and Marlena Brady Black. The biological family she had never known.

There were photos of Marlena's twins with Roman Brady, Sami and Eric, from the time they were toddlers to shots taken in the past year. Eric was always shown with family or a group of friends; he'd never married. Sami was with several hunks, undoubtedly each her husband at one time or another, and her three adorable children. Charley had heard that Sami was not only fascinating but had a checkered past, and she wondered if the two of them had anything remotely in common.

She turned the page to see photos of Carrie and Austin Reed. As Sami's half sister by Roman Brady, Carrie had become part of John and Marlena's extended family and was as close to them as their own children. Carrie had a beautiful smile. And by the way Austin held her in the photo, Charley knew they were in love. The kind of love she hoped she'd have one day.

With Brendan the fox? she thought. Then she shook her head and went back to looking at the photos.

Brady Black, John's oft-troubled son with Isabella Toscana, was strapping and gorgeous. He looked like someone Chance and Jackson would like to know.

And then there was Belle. Beautiful, blonde Belle was the only other biological child of both of the people whose genes flowed through Charley's body.

Charley had met Belle in Monte Carlo. In fact, Belle's loving husband, Shawn, had brought Marlena into Charley's life. Charley smiled as she thought about him. When they'd first met, the handsome sailor had dazzled Charley. He had even donated blood to her after the accident that had killed her mother and seriously injured her. Ironically, Shawn and Belle had been the ones who called Marlena to help Charley in the aftermath of the tragedy. The three of them already had a bond that none of the others could understand.

Belle had discovered she was pregnant about that time, and Shawn had been over the moon, as was their adorable almost-four-year-old moppet, Claire.

A niece or nephew, Charley realized. Soon she was going to actually be an aunt—again. A biological one, in any case.

She moved slowly from page to page, finding that each one held a story. Every one of them was fascinating to the girl who'd been avoiding them.

Finally, she reached the last page of the book. It was empty, but it still had a page number and the header that read "Our Loving Family." It held a handwritten inscription. Charley hesitated a moment before she read it.

"Charley, This page is held for the time you wish to be included in our extended and sometimes crazy family, should you ever decide to do so. In the meantime, we wanted you to get a glimpse of who we are to better help you know who you are or can be. Merry Christmas."

It was simply signed "John and Marlena."

The alarm went off next to Charley's bed, startling her. She realized she had been poring through the album for nearly two and a half hours.

Charley hadn't had a wink of sleep, but there in the still of the night in darkest Africa, she'd been given glimpses into John and Marlena's trials, tribulations, and heroics. As she began to get dressed, calmness came over her. For the first time, she felt she was beginning to understand a bit about them and the new cast of characters in her life.

Maybe the worst is behind us, she thought. Maybe life can be good again after all.

34  *ABBY*

THE MAHIKI LOUNGE WAS A FAVORITE OF THE ÜBER-TRENDY, über-wealthy, and über-chic set, especially during the bleak, blustery London winters. For those who could afford it, this sumptuous and exotic tiki bar in Mayfair was like an undiscovered private island. Bamboo walls, tiki torches, and rattan furniture added to the Polynesian ambiance.

Abby was, of course, a regular.

Fruit drinks with paper umbrellas had always been one of her favorites, and the piña coladas in pineapples at Mahiki were her poison. But tonight, with the love of her life joining her and four carats on her left hand, she ordered the Lover's Cup.

Jackson was more of a straight scotch kind of guy, but when he saw the massive pink drink for two filled with tropical fruit and orchids on the table, he indulged her. The day had been confusing for him since their lunch at Soho House and the unexpected call from Charley. Thankfully, Abby had let the Scarlett debacle drop.

"Hey." She smiled as he plopped beside her in the high-backed green booth overlooking the dance floor below. The room was already filled with London's elite.

"Hey, Gorgeous," he said and smiled back. Abby did have an engaging smile, and her eyes sparkled. She was a woman in love.

She leaned in for a kiss, and he accommodated her. Her lips were inviting and warm, and she nibbled his top lip sensuously.

His body tingled, radiating from his pelvis and reaching from his toes to the top of his head. It startled him and he pulled back.

"What's wrong?" Abby asked.

"Nothing," he said. But the tilt of his head made her pull back. "Really," he insisted. "Actually something's very right."

Jackson took her left hand in his. "It's more right than I expected."

"I guess that's a compliment." Abby smiled.

"I feel like I've been pulled out of hell and landed in paradise," he admitted.

"It's the tiki torches," Abby answered.

"No, it's you," Jackson corrected her.

"To us," she said, handing him one of the long straws from their oversized cocktail.

As Jackson took a long, sweet sip from the rum concoction, he spotted Chance on the first floor. His brother was alone, which was unusual for him at this time of the night. Chance was scouring the club for something. He moved through the gyrating dancers but ignored them all.

"Little brother's here," he said to Abby, indicating Chance in the crowd.

Jackson let out a quick whistle with hopes of getting his brother's attention. Abby had a better idea. She fished an ice cube from her frothy bowl and targeted her future brother-in-law. The wet square hit him right on his shoulder.

Chance looked up to see the lovers waving him up to join them. He shook his head no and pointed for Jackson to join him instead.

"Well, this could be interesting," Jackson said to Abby. "Be right back. I hope."

Abby nodded as Jackson left the banquette.

Abby took it all in. The music was pulsating, the crowd enthusiastic. She rested her chin in her hands, elbows on the table. Suddenly she realized it was vibrating.

Jackson had left his phone on the table. It was on silent mode, and someone was calling.

Abby reached for it but then pulled back. It was nearly three in the morning, so who would be calling? Answering someone else's phone, especially her fiancé's, would be an invasion of privacy, and she knew better.

The vibrating stopped and she stared at the phone for a long moment.

She could see Jackson and Chance below engaged in deep conversation.

Finally, call it reporter's instincts or impulse, but she couldn't help herself. She picked up Jackson's phone and saw there was a new voicemail. Against her better judgment, she listened.

"Hey, lover, when you get a chance, call me..."

Abby clicked off the phone and was heartsick. She didn't dare hear any more. She couldn't resist seeing who it was from, though, so she quickly scanned Jackson's recent calls. It was the same number she'd seen earlier: Royal Londolani.

Her heart sank. She knew it was Scarlett.

∞

On the floor below, Jackson was being given bad news.

"This has got to be a nightmare," Jackson groaned. "Someone wake me up!"

"You're as awake as I am, bruv," Chance said as he pinched his brother hard. "We're still on the hook legally for some of the money Dad swindled, so our flats are going on the auction block."

"When?" Jackson sighed.

"We have thirty days to get out," Chance said as he handed an envelope to his beloved brother. "And any gifts from Mum and Dad have to be turned over."

Now Jackson was the one who was heartsick and very, very confused.

He ran his hand through his dark brown mane as he tried to grasp the reality. He tipped his head back and caught sight of Abby looking down at him and Chance from her perch.

She blew him a kiss with her left hand.

Mum's ring, Jackson thought as his mind started swirling. Bloody hell.

35  *2:30 A.M.*

A DENSE BREEZE WAS ROLLING THROUGH THE DARKNESS OF THE Timbavati. Throughout the bush, exotic animals foraged for food. While elephants picked at brush and branches, hippos wallowed in shallow mud eating sticks and leaves. A pack of multicolored wild dogs ripped the flesh from a fallen gazelle several miles away, their howling and piercing barks celebrating their catch. Leaves rustled and snapped as antelopes scampered through the terrain.

Then a muffled shot rang out from a Browning A–Bolt.

What sounded like a trumpet blare indicated that the prey had been hit.

A gloved hand reloaded the rifle. Then another muffled shot blasted out of the gun barrel.

The pattern was repeated, and after one more shot there was a groaning sound and a heavy thud. Then a squeak like a wail.

"Shit," the shooter said.

Rustling could be heard nearby before another shot was loaded and another target hit.

There was another thud, but this one was not as heavy.

The breathing of the man behind the gun was heavy, though. Labored and anxious.

"Make sure they're dead," the hushed Afrikaans voice demanded. "But hurry."

Black hands took a hatchet from the truck and then hacked at the animals with intensity. Within minutes, two rhino horns had been severed. One was half the size of the other.

A mother rhino and her calf were dead, their carcasses left for the scavengers.

∞

The sound of the vehicle's engine stopped ten feet from the Falcon 200 parked on the Royal Londolani landing strip. An African tracker unloaded four cardboard boxes from the rear of the vehicle while the driver waited.

One by one, he took the precious treasures to the foot of the private jet's stairs.

He waited until a man appeared in the open doorway up top and nodded.

One by one, he brought the boxes up the stairs and into the cabin.

After a moment, the driver appeared behind him. With an X-Acto knife, he swiftly cut open each of the boxes.

Each one held an African white rhino horn, severed at the base. One remarkably smaller than the others.

"What's this?" Wen asked, pointing at the small horn.

"Didn't see the calf at first," Cornelius answered.

"Pity," Wen scowled. "Worth a third of what it would have gotten two years from now."

And that was a barrel of money.

36   *THE WATERING HOLE*

AFTER TOSSING AND TURNING FOR HOURS, SCARLETT HAD just drifted into a dream when Charley gently shook her.

"Shit!" Scarlett screamed as she pulled off her eye mask and tried to get her bearings. "What the hell time is it?" she gasped, breathing heavily. It was still very, very dark outside.

"Three-fifteen," Charley said. "We gave you as much time as we could since you're the senior girl."

Since I'm the old hag, Scarlett thought. At least there are some benefits.

"I'll be out in ten. Do you mind?" she sniped at Charley.

"I'm just doing my job, Scarlett," Charley answered gently. "Just get out as soon as you can, okay?"

Scarlett was surprised at how nice Charley was being. Charley was, too. But even though Charley had probably had even less sleep than Scarlett, she was feeling good about life this morning. Whether that was because of the glow she'd felt from the moment she'd met Brendan or the renewed sense of peace she'd found by going through the Black family history, she felt centered for the first time in months.

"But Vince'll be in soon," Charley purred, "so you may want to—"

"Get my ass in gear," Scarlett said appreciatively, completing Charley's thought.

∞

While magazine covers and photo layouts are always sleek and glossy, and the aura around all areas of the media is one of glamour and luxury, the truth behind it all is good, old-fashioned hard work.

Three a.m. makeup calls. Hours in a makeup chair making sure every flaw is corrected and every pore diminished. People poking and prodding while the art director or photographer looks at the models and actors under a microscope as though they're merely canvases on which to create an artistic vision.

And they are. Commodities. Highly paid and often pampered, not because of who they are, but because of what they are. And, more often than not, with a frighteningly short shelf life, the expiration date stamped in their minds like a tattoo.

Under the remarkable artistry of Greg, Alex, and Ashley, the models were ready to head to the shoot in a little under two hours.

The models wore their own casual wear as their guides led them to the Rovers that would take them to the watering hole. The terrain was wild and the ride incredibly bumpy. The night stars were still out, the only light except for the headlights on their vehicles. Now and again, wild animals scurried across the vehicles' path, and the drivers deftly avoided them as if they'd driven this obstacle course hundreds of times.

It took twenty-five minutes to arrive at the base camp near the watering hole. With a tracker to guide them, they would travel to a location that was out of the way of animal trails and downwind from where predators were expected to be. A game ranger could be seen sitting in the production van. That was standard procedure for any location shoot in the veld, to make sure every safety precaution was followed. Above all, the tourist board wanted to make sure every vacationer who visited the country left there in one piece to regale their friends about this land of wonder.

The two Rovers pulled into the site just before 5:00 a.m. Sunrise was scheduled for 5:21 so they only had twenty minutes to get the models into the swimsuits they'd sifted through the night before. Headlights lit the area.

Charley, in her lightweight khaki shorts and short-sleeved shirt, jumped out of the first Rover and headed to the van. When the door opened, she gasped.

"Morning," Brendan said, smiling.

"I—thought you had today off," Charley stammered.

Don't let me drool…don't let me drool…don't let me drool.

"I switched shifts with one of the girls," he said. "She wasn't feeling well this morning so I volunteered to cover for her."

So it wasn't to see me, Charley thought glumly.

"Great." she smiled wanly. "Now, we need to get in here."

"Right," Brendan said as he stared at her. Something in Charley's eyes mesmerized him. He wiped at the corners of his mouth.

He's not drooling, is he? Charley asked herself, hoping it was true.

"Ahem," they heard from behind her.

"We need to get in there." Scarlett smiled, cocking her head. "Unless you want to explain to Vince why we couldn't get ready."

∞

Ashley and her assistant headed into the changing area, and the girls changed into their bikinis. They'd each done this a hundred times, Scarlett a thousand, so it was quick and easy.

By the time they emerged, the sun was just beginning to peek over the horizon with shafts of coral, orange, and pink streaking the blackness. It was a glorious sight as the morning came alive, revealing dozens of the most exotic animals on the planet moving toward the massive watering hole, which was surrounded by a smattering of lush trees. Hippos, giraffes, kudus, and wildebeests all drank from the same well.

The girls piled out of the van, all barefoot and equally glorious. Brigitta wore a shimmering silver Dolce & Gabbana thong with a barely-there top that showed the outline of her nipples. Nikki was in a deep golden one-piece with the back cut down to the base of her spine. Scarlett shone in copper that added fire to her leonine red mane.

Vince was setting his camera as Charley positioned the girls. Brigitta on the ground resting her slightly tipped head on her elbow, Nikki kneeling behind her, and Scarlett in an elegant pose reaching for the sky. They undulated slightly at Vince's command, the animals oblivious to the action.

Charley was taking notes and making adjustments as Vince directed.

"Suggestion?" Charley asked.

"Go for it," Vince answered.

"Scarlett in front, Brigitta in the rear," she offered. "The color palette's better."

"Once again, right," Vince admitted. "Girls, let's give Charley's idea a shot."

Nikki and Brigitta were fine with the repositioning. Scarlett was not. She knew the attention would go to the leggy blonde, and she was pissed. She stood stock-still and glared.

"You okay with this, Scarlett?" Vince asked with a tone that said she'd better be.

"No!" she barked back in a tone that even startled her. "I am not fine with her constant interference, Vince! She hates me. You know that, don't you?"

"She has a fabulous eye," he snapped. "And you're being the egotistical bitch that nearly killed your reputation, Scarlett!"

"Her brother's the guy I dumped when I went back to you, and she's taking it out on me."

Vince's teeth clenched and his fist pumped.

"That was fucking ten years ago," he spewed. "Now move your bony ass."

They were nearly now nose to nose.

"I'll move it all right," she glared and then turned on her heel and stomped away from him toward the bushes that rimmed the watering hole.

"Get back here!" he shouted.

"I need five. Everyone take five!" Scarlett screamed as she kept moving.

Nikki and Brigitta rose from their positions, while Ashley, Greg, and Alex shared looks of disgust at Scarlett's tantrum.

"The sun's changing every second, Scarlett," Vince warned.

"Five!" Scarlett demanded again as she waved him off dismissively.

"We may need ten, Vince," Charley shrugged. They did need to stay on schedule, but Charley recognized a stone wall when she saw one.

"Ten minutes," Vince growled, thrusting his hands through his hair and heading to the van.

"I'll see what I can do," Charley called after him apologetically.

"Somehow, I don't think her seeing you is going to help," Nikki said from behind her.

"Or you," Brigitta said to Nikki, remembering how threatened Scarlett had been when Cornelius flirted with Nikki and not her. "I'll get her back," she said, smiling innocently.

Before Charley could object, Brigitta headed after their petulant coworker.

Charley sighed heavily. She turned to see Brendan staring straight at her. Even with three of the most glamorous women in the world nearly naked in front of him, and all the chaos, his eyes were only on her.

Charley felt her face flush as he smiled. But the moment was broken by a blood-curdling scream.

Brendan snapped back to see Scarlett at the base of one of the low-hanging trees, staring horrified into the bush. Brigitta was several feet in front of her. Behind them, the animals began to stir.

"Everyone move slowly but quickly to the Rovers," Brendan commanded calmly. "Girls, that means you."

Scarlett backed away, shaking like a leaf as the others moved to the protection of the cars. Then she turned quickly and bolted, running smack into Brigitta. As if in slow motion, Brigitta tumbled to the ground, her arms flailing as her head landed with a crack on a large boulder.

Everything stopped.

Scarlett was in shock, and Brigitta was out cold.

Brendan swiftly moved to the model's side.

"Everyone stay back," he said.

He checked her over quickly but efficiently. She was still breathing but foggy when she was asked her name and where she was. Her bell had been rung badly, and her face was red and swelling.

"We need to get her to a hospital," Charley said.

"No, I think I'm okay," Brigitta insisted. "Really. Just need to rest a little."

"Let's get someone to the game farm to check her over," Brendan said. "If you can call our friends at Tom-Ali."

"Doesn't anyone care about me?" they heard behind them. Scarlett was frozen in place, her translucent skin paler than ever.

"Come on, Scarlett, Brigitta," Charley said as she led them both to the production van.

With the sun filtering light across the bush, Brendan moved to investigate the situation. Just out of view of the others he saw what Scarlett had faced: two dead white rhino, a mother and her calf. Their horns were severed and blood stained their cheeks like red tears. The meat on their carcasses had been nearly stripped clean.

37  *BILL AND CORNELIUS*

IT WAS JUST AFTER 8:00 A.M. WHEN CORNELIUS PULLED THE VAN into the gravel parking lot of Tom-Ali. He'd had an exhausting night and had only caught a few hours of sleep before heading to the clinic. Bill was due in at nine, and patients would be lining up soon for their free services.

Kayla and Marlena would also be arriving before long for their trip to the Mapusha weavers. They would want to be on the road as early as possible to make the forty-five minute trek to the weavers' village of Rooiboklaagte, since the heat would become brutal as it neared noon. They would be taking the van so Cornelius had to make sure there were no telltale signs of his butchery.

Cornelius turned off the engine and checked his reflection in the rearview mirror.

A million rand. Not bad, he thought. In U.S. dollars that's nearly a hundred fifty thousand. Before long I'll have enough to retire in St. Thomas. Too bad about that calf...

In the sliver of the mirror, he could see what appeared to be patients approaching in the distance behind him. Their ages were indeterminable, but one was shuffling and the other had his arm in a sling. Cornelius pulled the gun from under the passenger's seat and then went to the rear door of the clinic and opened it with his key.

∞

Bill was startled to see Cornelius enter. But he was not as startled as Cornelius was to see him.

"Mornin'," Bill said.

"Same," Cornelius answered. "How are you feeling?"

"Better than most, not as good as some," Bill lied. The truth was that he was feeling worse than usual. Listless, he could feel his hands trembling and his stomach churning.

"What's up?" Cornelius said as casually as he could. "Didn't expect to see you so early."

"Wanted to check inventory," Bill said. "Make sure we have enough to cover Kayla's trip to Rooiboklaagte. We're tight."

"I stocked the van yesterday."

Bill looked relieved.

"But I get it. I'm really sorry about the financial mess," Cornelius said.

The truth was that Cornelius was thrilled everything was falling apart. He'd been up to his hips in the rhino-poaching scandal for more than six months and knew the heat was on.

"Thanks for not telling anyone," Bill answered. "Unfortunately Patch found out, but he swears he won't tell Kayla yet."

Good deal, Cornelius thought. Everyone's learning you're in deep and need cash—several hundred thousand dollars—or the clinic is history.

"Let me put this away, and I'll give you a hand," Cornelius said casually.

For the first time, Bill noticed the Browning A-Bolt.

"Is that mine?" he said.

He'd been so wrapped up in his own worries that he barely noticed anything anymore. Besides, the Rohypnol Cornelius had dropped into last night's Carling Black Label was still in his system.

"You asked me to have it cleaned," Cornelius lied as he presented the rifle to Bill. "Before the holiday, remember?"

Bill shook his head slowly as Cornelius handed him the rifle. "No, I don't. When?"

"Bill, I'm getting worried here," Cornelius said, dodging the question. "Just after Christmas. We were discussing security, and you wanted to make sure we had it covered. Do you really not remember?"

Bill turned the gun over in his hands several times, straining to remember. His brow furled as he tried to remember but couldn't—because it wasn't true. Before Bill could answer, there was a knocking on the door.

"I saw them headed toward us when I parked. It's a young Xhosa with his arm in a makeshift sling. Let me put that in the back and wash up," Cornelius said as he indicated Bill's rifle.

"Thanks," was all Bill could say as he handed the gun back to Cornelius. The gun with his fresh fingerprints all over it.

"Then I'll make sure the van's ready to go," Cornelius answered as he headed to the storage room.

"Thanks," Bill said again solemnly as he went to let in the first patient.

Bill was befuddled, and Cornelius knew it.

Like taking candy from a baby, Cornelius thought, smiling to himself as he disappeared into the storage room. *A very big, very drugged baby.*

∞

By the time Patch pulled into the lot and parked next to Bill's car, a line had formed in the waiting pen. The rear doors of the Jeep opened and Kayla got out first, releasing the straps on Joe's car seat as he squirmed.

Patch and Marlena climbed out of the front.

"Thank you so much for picking me up," Marlena said, smiling.

"Did we have a choice?" Patch joked.

"Steve!" Kayla said, reprimanding him. "We could have said no, rather than all three of us showing up."

Patch and Kayla had joined Marlena and John for a lavish breakfast in the lapa of the Royal Londolani before the day started. The owner and his wife were two of the top chefs in South Africa, and their meals were legendary. The Royal Londolani was known for having the most scrumptious meals in the area, if not in most of South Africa, especially breakfast. They offered wild boar steaks and the freshest eggs, fruits, freshly baked breads, and croissants that would make a Frenchman jealous. When John invited Patch and Kayla, there was no way they could or would say no.

It had been a beautiful way to start a day that would take Marlena to one of her favorite places in the area.

"Sorry that John's not going with us," Patch said to Marlena as they approached the front door.

Marlena wasn't. She would love to have John visit the synergy project that had become so important to Patch and Kayla, but when she and John were together, her focus was laser sharp on him. Today Bill needed her; Patch and Kayla needed her; and the project needed her. And she needed time on her own.

When they entered the clinic, Bill was at the desk going over a list of the day's patients with Beauty and another young Xsoha who was volunteering. They knew nearly everyone who showed up at their door from the small town and the surrounding area.

"Well, hi all." Bill smiled as Joe headed for the small candy bowl in front of him and dove right in.

"One piece, Joe Johnson," Kayla cautioned as the others said hello.

"Only one?" Joe said with pleading eyes on Bill.

"One for now, and maybe one for later," he answered. "But only if your mommy and daddy say it's okay." Being brought up a well-mannered Horton, Bill still held fast to the idea that parents have the final say.

Joe stared at his father with his big, blue eyes. "Okay, one for now, and one for later, Bud."

"Softy," Kayla said, shaking her head.

Joe popped the candy in his pocket and started running from room to room.

"Where's Cornelius?" Kayla asked.

"Gassing up the van," Bill informed her.

"Then could we take twenty minutes, you and me?" Marlena asked Bill.

"Want to check my brain?" Bill responded. They had worked

together off and on so many times that they understood each other's shorthand.

"Well, yes," she said simply and smiled. Marlena's smile was as warm as it had been the first time he'd met her.

"I may be crazy these days, but I'm not stupid," Bill responded wryly. He glanced at Kayla and gave her a knowing look. "I know how close you two are, Kayla, and I don't blame you for being concerned. I am, too."

"It's been a little scary," Kayla admitted.

"If we leave in thirty, we'll be fine," Patch said. "I can run this little guy around outside for a few," he said as Joe ran past him.

"Good idea," Kayla nodded.

"Let's use one of the exam rooms," Bill said as he led Marlena to the back. "I need some answers."

∞

"It is good to see you, Bill," Marlena said as he took a seat across from her in a room that was spare but functional.

"I've had incredible pressures, Marlena," Bill admitted.

"Want to tell me about them?" she asked.

Bill studied the woman he respected so highly and knew at this point he had doctor-patient privilege. But the stubborn male pride he'd been famous for in Salem wouldn't let him admit his folly.

"The economy sucks," is all he said. "But that doesn't explain my memory lapses."

"You know the drill, I'm sure."

Bill nodded, and Marlena took a pad and pencil from her handbag.

"Let's start with me giving you a list. Then I want you to say it out loud, and I'll ask for it again later."

He nodded again.

"Candle, pencil, fire engine…" she said as she began the standard memory tests for dementia and Alzheimer's. Marlena knew Bill's family history well, and while his ex-wife had once been diagnosed with severe mental illness, there was none in the Horton lineage. That diagnosis was unlikely, but as a professional she had to check.

Bill passed with flying colors.

"I just keep forgetting things!" He was disgusted with himself. "Meetings, details, phone calls, things like that."

Actually, aside from his financial blunder, Bill was as sharp as a tack.

"How much have you been drinking?" Marlena asked matter-of-factly.

"No more than two beers a day, and usually not even that," he assured her.

Marlena was puzzled.

"Have you had a blood test recently?"

"Nope," Bill admitted.

"Well, if it's a chemical imbalance, that'll give us some answers," Marlena said with confidence as she made a note to ask Kayla or Cornelius to draw a blood panel.

"I hope so, Marlena," Bill said. "If I don't figure this out, I really will go crazy."

38  *SCARLETT*

MINIBARS HAD ALWAYS BEEN SCARLETT'S FRIENDS, AND THE fully stocked fridge in the bedroom of her suite was no exception.

The morning had been grueling, not only physically but also emotionally. The debacle at the watering hole had turned the entire shoot into upheaval. They had originally scheduled three days at Londolani and then had planned to go to Cape Point at the tip of the country, another dazzling location with enormous sea cliffs above the battering ocean. Then on to one of the clubs in Cape Town, followed by two days in the red sands of the Serengeti. But because of Brigitta's accident, everyone agreed that, for safety's sake, she should sit out the rest of the day and get some much-needed bed rest.

Rather than lose an entire morning of shooting, Charley suggested they could do what was known as guerilla shooting with Vince's second unit. The method, which was basically driving aimlessly until finding a spot that instilled inspiration, had succeeded wildly for Vince in his early days as a photographer.

Vince thought it was inspired thinking.

Charley was the golden girl once again.

And Scarlett would have none of it. She'd rather be shooting with real gorillas than be anywhere near Charley.

At that point, Vince would rather have had Scarlett anywhere but near them. So, when Brigitta was driven back to the game farm after her bruises were tended to, Scarlett went with her.

And there, in the privacy of her room, feeling a mixture of guilt and frustration, Scarlett got very friendly with her "mini-friends." Orange juice and vodka, cranberry juice and rum, tequila and ginger ale.

Yum, yum, and yum.

By 10:00 a.m. she was sloshed. She tried to sleep but couldn't. Between jet lag, lack of sleep, the experience at the watering hole, and too much alcohol, she was restless. So, she got up and poured herself another drink.

Maybe some fresh air will help.

Dressed in nothing but lightweight shorts and a cropped tank, Scarlett went out on the large wooden deck and looked out across the beautiful, peaceful terrain.

Looks like Santa Barbara, she thought. Someday I'll retire there with some handsome billionaire.

Taking a long deep breath, she started to cough. The heat and the alcohol were not a good mix.

The spa would be nice, she thought. A hot stone massage or a lymphatic drain. Maybe a facial! Damn, where is the spa?

Against all warnings, she took off to find it by herself.

The elevated wooden paths back to the lapa and the spa wound through the grounds, and Scarlett sipped on her gin and lemonade as she strolled them.

Down to the last of the glass, she saw two ice cubes stuck to the side and was determined to get them. She'd always loved to suck on ice and let it roll around in her mouth while it dissolved. It was a sensuous move that she used often on her sexual conquests.

Tipping her head back and tapping the fine cut-glass tumbler, Scarlett lost her balance and fell off the pathway. She landed face first in a puddle of slimy mud. She lay there a moment and then sat up. She was a mess. But instead of being furious, all Scarlett could do was laugh.

At least I didn't knock myself out, she thought.

Extricating herself from the slime, she looked around to see where she was.

Doesn't look so friggin' dangerous to me, she thought as she glanced around the area. Getting her bearings, she realized she could easily take a short cut across grassy paths to her salvation. That way, no one on the well-trodden path would see her covered in goo.

She carefully made her way through the foliage past the next private suite, all the while keeping out a keen eye for creatures.

Then she smelled something. An odor she knew well. Turning to look in the direction of the aroma, she spotted someone smoking a joint on the deck of the Xings' suite.

Never fearful, Scarlett made her way toward the pungent smell. The sound of her footsteps was masked by the sounds of small animals scurrying nearby.

"Do not kill a calf again, or we will have to sever our ties!"

Scarlett stopped dead in her tracks.

"It's never happened before and it will never happen again, I promise you."

Scarlett recognized the Afrikaans accent and the voice. *Cornelius.*

"The small horn is less than two pounds," Jiao-jie scolded. "You realize how much money you threw away by slaughtering that animal?"

"With an average horn weighing eight to ten—" he started.

"Close to a million dollars on the black market!" Jiao-jie snapped.

Scarlett dropped her glass in shock.

Cornelius turned to see her. While she was less than five feet away from the deck, no one else could see her. Before he could react, she put her hands to her lips, warning him to be quiet.

Something told him he should do it.

"We leave tomorrow," Jiao-jie said as she ended her diatribe. "Forty-thousand U.S. cash if you can deliver by takeoff."

Scarlett was not only drunk and covered in mud, but she was also dumbstruck.

"We have a car waiting now, so go," Jiao-jie said as she dismissed Cornelius with a wave of her hand.

He jumped down from the deck and moved toward the supermodel as they both heard Jiao-jie and Wen leave with their escort.

It seemed like an eternity before either of them spoke. Scarlett went first.

"Nice per-formance last night," she slurred. "Rhino poach-ing a bad, bad thing."

"You all seemed to buy my little speech," he countered as he noticed how wobbly she was. "And now you've heard how profitable it can be," he said, indicating the deck. "The Xings have made millions. And rhino? So what if they disappear?"

Scarlett's mind was muddled. She was terrified of the danger she'd stumbled into and desperate to find a way out.

"Then you'd be out of a job…" she smiled lazily.

Cornelius wasn't sure what to make of her.

"You're lucky Wen didn't see you, you know," Cornelius stated.

"And you're lucky you did," she smiled lazily.

"I could make you disappear faster than a hit off that joint," he reminded her.

"You wouldn't," she responded. She was terrified of his threat, but she knew she couldn't show any fear if she was going to get out of this. "Not when I can make you even more money."

"I'm listening…" he said.

"Rhin-o horn," she answered. "Who needs a middleman? Every supermodel in the world still wants it. I can get them to buy from us direct."

"Us."

"Us," she said confidently. "I'm the one with the connections."

Cornelius was impressed. This girl was not only hot, but she had nerve.

"You're smarter than you look, Ms. O'Hara," he chuckled. "Especially right now." He pointed at her mud-streaked face.

"Not the time to be funny, Mr.—"

"Bekker."

"Mr. Bekker." Scarlett was sobering up fast. "Do we have a deal?"

Cornelius studied her for a long moment.

"You're the perfect package, aren't you?"

"Some say. Deal?" she repeated firmly.

"Deal."

Scarlett put out her hand and Cornelius grabbed it firmly. Then he yanked her close and hungrily kissed the one clean and exposed side of her long neck.

"I'll watch you, now go!" he ordered. "I'll contact you," he said before releasing her.

Scarlett nodded quickly and then headed in the direction of the spa. From the look on his face, it was clear she needed a spa now more than ever.

39  JOHN

Stretching out between gnarled jackalberry and Acacia thorn trees, the spa at Londolani was created to encapsulate all the African experience has to offer. With the majestic sky as its ceiling and built around a courtyard with traditional African touches, the spa was as popular with some visitors as the magnificence of the bush.

John had opted to stay at the game farm after breakfast while Marlena traveled with Patch and Kayla to their volunteer project in Rooiboklaagte.

His rehabilitation had been complete for less than a year, and John was determined to stay in the best shape of his life. Not only for himself, but also for Marlena and the rest of his family. He owed them that.

John spent the morning in the state-of-the-art gym, adhering to the strict routine he'd followed since he'd passed his ISA endurance tests less than a year earlier. Then he took a vigorous swim in the 25-meter pool while he waited for a therapeutic massage by one of the finest internationally qualified therapists in the world.

John had just completed his twentieth lap when he noticed Scarlett entering through the Indian teakwood doors.

At least he thought the woman was Scarlett. She had that flowing red hair, but she was covered in mud.

Scarlett gasped when she saw John. She had expected the spa to be empty.

"You look like you've seen a ghost," John said as he picked up his towel from the chaise lounge nearby. "Or did you run into some ferocious creature?"

"I did." She nodded as she thought of Cornelius and his threat.

"What was it?"

Scarlett had a choice to make. She could spill everything to John or keep her full, pouty lips shut. She opted for the latter.

"I—don't know," she stammered. "It all happened so fast."

She wouldn't make eye contact with him. And if John had learned one thing in his training in the International Security Alliance, it was to recognize the signs of a liar.

"Let's get you cleaned up here," John said masterfully. Protecting a woman in need was woven into his DNA, and this was no exception.

The spa had a number of outdoor showers close by, so John strode to one and turned on the water. Scarlett stood under the cleansing flow as John removed the gooseneck showerhead and directed it over her body. The water washed away the grime from her hair, her face, and her shorts while the tank top clung to her breasts. John couldn't help but notice.

Scarlett looked up at John, and his blue eyes were inviting. Though John did not initiate or even invite it, she kissed him. Thoroughly.

Neither of them saw that Charley had just entered the spa.

Charley was horrified when she saw them. She ducked out of sight, nearly knocking over Tuma, who was behind her, before she saw John pull away.

Was he kissing her? she asked herself, trying to shake the image out of her head. Is he as bad a womanizer as Richie was? she wondered as she tried to catch her breath. She leaned against the back of the teak doorjamb.

"Are you all right, ma'am?" Tuma asked. "Do you need to sit down?"

"I'm just a little faint, Tuma," she said, trying to cover her shock.

"Let's get you something to eat, then." He smiled warmly.

She nodded weakly as he led her toward the dining room.

Her mind was whirling. *Is that happy family in the album really a lie?*

40  *ABBY AND JACKSON*

ABBY NESTLED IN JACKSON'S ARMS AS THEY LAY BETWEEN THE luxurious sheets in his massive bed. The morning light of London filtered through the bedroom window.

Abby had a contented smile on her face. Jackson just stared at the ceiling.

His mind had been whirling since Chance had given him the news at Mahiki. Unless there was a miracle, he'd lose his sanctuary within a month.

The alarm went off. Abby shifted her weight as her eyes slowly opened. Her fingers ran across Jackson's inviting lips.

"I love you," she whispered.

He looked at her and half smiled. She was truly beautiful when she woke up, one of those girls who didn't need makeup. He'd had plenty of the others over the years and had been shocked plenty of times, come the light of day.

"Thanks for last night," he said.

"My honor," she replied.

Jackson was starting to appreciate her more than ever. Abby

was a wonderful lover. She'd become one unexpectedly through her work. Her gossip site was always rife with indiscretions, divorces, and turmoil. So in true journalistic fashion, she had investigated everything she could about sex and relationships. Everything from studying the art of the geisha to reading *The New Joy of Sex* had turned Abby into a master. Now Jackson was reaping those benefits.

"'Morning, lover," Jackson said.

She sensed something in his tone, but she didn't want to ask. In fact she was afraid to, considering her growing insecurities about Scarlett.

"Coffee or cappuccino?"

"Coffee," he answered. "With—"

"Two sugars, I know," Abby said, smiling. "And fresh orange juice."

Jackson smiled. She seemed to know his every like and dislike, and she doted on him without smothering him. He knew this had to be hard for her, but she still seemed determined to make it work. Why? Maybe she truly loved him.

Abby slid out of bed and pulled Jackson's silk pajama top over her naked body. He appreciated the fact that she had so little pretense. As she headed out, she flipped her long, blonde waves to keep them from getting caught under the collar. It was a sensuous move, and she looked back as she exited.

But Jackson hadn't seen her. His mind was already elsewhere.

∞

Abby was pouring Jackson's coffee into a fine porcelain mug as he walked into the kitchen. He was wearing the matching pajama bottoms, and she smiled.

"You didn't have to get dressed for me," she said playfully as she took two cubes of raw sugar from the canister on the counter and plopped them into Jackson's mug. "I like naked."

"Me, too," he responded, trying to match her mood.

"And, while I love my soon-to-be sister-in-law, I have to admit I love having this place to ourselves more right now. Sex in any room without having to worry is quite liberating."

"As if you need liberating," Jackson answered, chuckling.

"At last."

"What?"

"I thought I saw a smile."

"Oh," he sighed deeply.

"Don't go serious on me this morning, Sugar," she begged.

"'Fraid I have to. Abby, we have to talk."

"We talk all the time," she answered, trying to lighten the moment.

"I'm serious."

"I'm warning you…" she said with a lilt in her voice.

The last thing Jackson wanted was this discussion, and that showed on his face.

"I don't know how else to say this—"

"Then don't—"

"But I have to have the ring back."

Abby's stomach caved in as if she'd been punched.

"I am so sorry…" he said as he reached out to her.

But at that moment, everything else in the world stopped for her. The deep, rapid thumping of her heart drowned out the rest of the words coming out of Jackson's mouth. If she could have listened, she'd have heard him explain the real reason he needed the ring back, and that he truly loved her and knew what having that ring meant to her. Like his mother's sapphire, which Prince William gave to Kate Middleton, Jackson's mother's ring was more special than any newly bought diamond.

But she didn't hear him. Instead, she lashed out.

"My dad was right, dammit," Abby said as she started to boil. "You *are* a no-good playboy who can't get a job because of his family's reputation."

Jackson was stung.

"On top of that, you're a liar!"

"What—?"

Abby ripped the ring off her left hand and threw it at him. Jackson caught it in midair.

"I knew you were still in love with her!"

She stormed out of the kitchen, leaving Jackson stunned. He stared at the ring. It felt as though it was burning through his hand.

"What? Who am I still in love with?" Then it dawned on him, and he ran after her.

Abby was madly pulling her slim dress over her head as Jackson entered the bedroom.

"We need to talk," Jackson insisted.

"We did talk. Now go away!" she spewed as she fastened the zipper. "I knew it was over when you didn't say 'I love you' back! I am such a fool!" She grabbed her cashmere sweater from the back of the lounge chair.

"Abby—" Jackson said as he moved toward her.

"Stay back, and you just keep your lying little paws off me!"

"I never lied! Do you think I'm in love with Scarlett O'Hara?"

"Yes, or is there someone else?" Abby demanded to know.

"No. And no!" Jackson said, defending himself. "I don't believe this is happening."

"Believe it," Abby snapped as she grabbed her coat from the back of his Eames chair. "I've made a lot of mistakes in my life, but I've never been such a fool!"

Before Jackson could stop her, she was gone.

41 *MAPUSHA WEAVERS SYNERGY CO-OP*

THE TOM-ALI MEDICAL VAN PULLED AWAY FROM THE CLINIC with five eager passengers. Patch drove with Marlena next to him. Kayla stayed in the back with little Joe and Beauty, who had come along as their interpreter.

The drive to the tiny village of Rooiboklaagte took about forty-five minutes. They passed through territory that reminded Marlena of the trips she used to take with her family when she was growing up in Colorado. The Drakensberg range was on one side with the lowlands nestled against its mountains. Low scrub brush dotted the area, as well as a smattering of trees.

Leading into the village, the area was dotted with small concrete houses with well-raked yards and gardens filled with vegetables. Churches were scattered through the village. Chickens and children and goats scattered everywhere.

"What's the population now?" Marlena asked as she glanced at the rural community.

"About two thousand, I'd guess," Patch answered. "At least half of them little kids."

The African population was growing disproportionately, and the rate of life-threatening disease was climbing with it. An estimated thirty percent of the people or more were HIV positive.

"Are they all here?" Marlena asked when she saw dozens and dozens of colorfully dressed Africans anxiously awaiting their arrival.

"They obviously got the word out that we were coming," Patch said as he pulled the van into the tiny village.

"And look at those shining faces," Marlena said, emotion overtaking her.

"We're the last hope for some of them," Kayla reminded her. "It's why they come out to see us so eagerly."

Neither woman noticed Patch's reaction. The secret he held about Tom-Ali's imminent financial collapse was weighing on him. He knew that if the clinic folded, there would be little hope for many of these people.

"We see reports on the news all the time at home, but until you're actually here, you don't really feel it," Marlena said, taking a deep sigh. "The energy is just incredible."

"Speaking of energy, I think Joe's ready to explode," Kayla said. After an hour in the backseat, Joe was antsier than ever.

"Stopping now, Sweetness," Patch said as he parked next to the building that served as the artisan studio. The exterior walls were painted with murals and were a rotating canvas for the villagers. "Everybody out!"

The patients' eager anticipation energized the group emerging from the van as much as the most potent drugs they'd brought with them. Joe jumped out and headed straight for the children who were playing everywhere. He was immediately lost in the sea of colored garments, many of which had been crafted nearby.

"Be careful!" Kayla called to him as he scampered off in the direction of a group of boys playing happily with used Popsicle sticks and threadbare soccer balls.

"Don't worry, Sweetness. I'll watch him," Patch assured her.

Patch kept one eye on Joe as he released the latch that opened the side canopy of the van. In the intense sun of South African summer, the shade was welcome.

Two of the women from the Mapusha Weavers Synergy Co-op emerged from the main building. Gertrude was the eldest of the cooperative and their master weaver, and Angy, one of the youngest weavers, was known for her use of vivid colors. The two women brought their visitors tall pitchers of iced tea. Their smiles matched those of the children.

"Welcome," said Gertrude with a thick African accent.

"Welcome," echoed Angy. They both prided themselves on having learned a few words of English.

"How is your husband?" Kayla said, as they began to catch up. Beauty translated as Kayla asked questions and Marlena drank it all in. She learned that Gertrude's elderly husband still tended gardens and that their thirteen grandchildren were all in school. Angy was hoping to move closer to the compound, but she still walked an hour each day to create amazing multicolored tapestries and rugs that were wildly popular with the tourists.

What Angy earned there helped support her blind father and unemployed brother as well as the other members of her family. Jobs were scarce everywhere in the world, but nowhere more scarce than in Africa. The women who'd created this project were supporting not only themselves but also their community.

For nearly three hours, Marlena and Kayla listened to the stories of the ailing and needy who arrived by the dozens at the mobile van. At the same time, the two friends provided medicines for the villagers' illnesses and compassion for their souls. Parents brought small children to be tested for malaria and TB. Patients of all ages underwent HIV testing and received ARV drugs, while others were given antibiotics to fight off fevers and infection.

All the while, Land Rovers from nearby game farms arrived for tours and to witness the artistry of the women who'd created their own future.

The last patient was a pregnant young girl named Lindah who could have been no more than thirteen. She had walked more than two hours in the blistering heat to see them.

"How far along is she?" Kayla asked Beauty. She asked Lindah and translated the reply. Kayla and Marlena listened, sickened, as Lindah told Beauty the story of how she had been raped six months ago by an uncle.

Her uncle had AIDS and was one who still believed that raping a virgin could cure him. That had been a common belief for years in many of the rural villages and accounted for a tremendous amount of tragedy. Lindah now feared that she was HIV positive and prayed she had not infected her unborn child.

"We can test you and have the results back in a few days," Kayla told her. "Until then, we will all pray for you and your baby."

Kayla had been raised a staunch Roman Catholic and still believed in the power of prayer. She had to.

Beauty translated, and Lindah nodded her thanks. Then Beauty saw Patch signaling her and went to join him.

Kayla checked Lindah's vitals and took blood samples. When she was finished, Marlena enveloped the frightened young girl in her arms and held her tightly.

Kayla fought back tears but was jolted back to reality when she heard Joe calling her from across the road.

"Mommy, look!" he shouted excitedly. "To infinity and beyond!"

Joe was standing on a five-foot-high cinder-block wall, and Kayla was horrified. "Joseph Johnson, you get down from there!" she called.

With arms outstretched and emulating his favorite Buzz Lightyear, Joe flung himself into the air.

"Joe!" Kayla screamed as the little boy landed in the rock-hard dirt below.

"Owwwwwww!" His scream could have shattered glass.

Kayla ran toward him as Joe started wailing and clutching his right arm. She could see blood gushing from a gaping wound just below his right wrist.

One of the African boys got to Joe first and reached out to help him. Kayla could see the boy had scraped knees and fingers from playing in the dirt.

"You stay back. Do not touch him!" Kayla yelled in a panic.

The boy stumbled back as Kayla literally pushed him aside.

"What is the matter with you, Joe Johnson!" she scolded. "What were you thinking? Let me see your arm. Steve!" she screamed. He was nowhere in sight. "Steven!"

"It was the tokoloshi," Joe wailed. "They pushed me!"

He was sobbing, his wrist limp and blood gushing through a tear in his flesh.

"Stop lying about that, Joe!" Kayla barked. Then she caught herself and attempted to calm down. "You'll be all right," she said. "You'll be in a cast, but you'll be all right."

"Sweet Lord," she heard as Steve dashed toward them from the main studio.

"Where were you?" Kayla snapped. "You said you'd watch him!"

She was furious; Joe was crying; and Patch was now angry, too. "I had to take a leak, and Beauty said she'd watch him."

From behind a large tree nearby, they both saw Beauty emerge with a handsome young boy about her age. She stood frozen, realizing what had happened.

"Joe, I am sorry," Patch said, trying to console his son. "But you're a tough guy, right? A broken bone or two when you're a kid makes you tougher."

"Help me get him to the van," Kayla said, glaring at her husband. "We'll get some X rays and see what we've got." She breathed deeply, determined to let her professional side take over and to calm down for Joe's sake. But her blood was boiling.

She was also feeling guiltier than she had in ages. She didn't want to admit it to herself, but she knew why.

"Hold it as still as you can, baby," she directed her son. "And let Daddy carry you."

Patch picked up his whimpering son as gently as he could, while Kayla had Joe place his right arm over his left for support.

"What were you doing anyway, pal?" Patch asked as he carried Joe to the van.

"It was the tokoloshi," Joe insisted.

"You cannot blame them for everything, Joe," Kayla said, more frustrated than angry.

"Think we've been in Africa a bit too long?" Patch said under his breath as they walked through the crowd of onlookers.

"No," Kayla insisted as she passed Marlena and Lindah.

But in her heart, Kayla wondered if he was right.

∞

The forty-five minute ride back to Tom-Ali was agonizing for everyone. Kayla had made a makeshift splint out of tongue depressors wrapped tightly with gauze and cold packs. She had also given Joe pediatric morphine to ease his discomfort. But the constant jarring from the rutted roads kept him whimpering.

"We'll be there soon," Kayla whispered gently in his ear, though she knew that wasn't true.

Joe put the thumb from his left hand in his mouth and began sucking it for comfort.

"It'll be all right, baby. I promise."

Her instinct was to rock him, but she knew better. She just held him gently and rested her head on his. Within a few minutes, his whimpering stopped as he fell asleep in her arms.

"A mother's touch," Marlena said, as she watched her friend cradle her son.

"No casting bandages," Kayla said quietly. "Cornelius was supposed to stock everything. He should be shot."

"Joe will be all right," Marlena assured her gently. "You know that."

Kayla nodded. "I do. But protecting and nurturing your children is the most important job in the world," she said softly. "You know that."

"When they're Joe's age, sometimes they even let you," Marlena said, looking away with her thoughts going to her own children.

Kayla saw Marlena's expression change and knew what it meant. "How's it going with Charley?" she asked.

"She's not our daughter but she is," Marlena answered. "That biological connection is actually stronger than even I'd realized."

"Nature versus nurture is still a mysterious thing," Kayla said. "Whether Charley likes it or not, there's a lot of you both in her. And she shouldn't just like that, she should be thrilled."

"Maybe one day she will be," Marlena said appreciatively as she glanced out across the passing scenery. "Maybe one day she will be."

42 VINCE, CHARLEY, AND BRENDAN

Soft, rhythmic African music played through the sound system as Tuma escorted a shell-shocked Charley into the lapa.

Vince sat on one of the white down sofas in the elegantly appointed open room. He was going through the morning's shots on his Mac as they entered.

"I thought you were getting a massage, kiddo," Vince said as he saw her approach.

"I changed my mind," she said, jolted back to reality. "And thank you, Tuma," she added.

"Nothing to eat?" Tuma asked.

"No, no, thank you. I just needed air. I'll be fine," she said, forcing a smile.

"I will be at reception if you need me." He answered with his engaging smile and started to exit.

"Wait, Tuma," Vince said, stopping him. He turned to Charley. "Go back to the spa. I don't offer these perks very often, and you saved the day with that suggestion about guerilla shooting, Charley. We got some damned good stuff."

"Which means we have work to do," she insisted.

Vince leaned back and studied his potential protégée as she sat next to him. "Okay, but now and then you need to relax."

"I'm fine," she insisted more firmly.

"If you don't mind my mentioning it, you're not," he offered. "But if you'd rather be working, who am I to stop you?"

Vince nodded to Tuma, who left them alone. Vince could see that Charley was fighting back tears.

"Want to tell me what's going on?" His voice was calm and his demeanor professional, which surprised her.

"Could I just see the shots again?" she asked, dodging his questions. Seeing John and Scarlett had made her especially vulnerable. The lack of sleep and the intense midday heat didn't help.

"Sure, but let me get you something to drink," he said, standing.

"Nonalcoholic," she insisted. "And thanks."

Vince went to the open bar and poured Charley some ice water, plopped in a few cucumber slices, and returned with the glass.

"I am truly grateful you said yes to this gig," he said as he watched her drink the cooling liquid.

"How could I say no?" she answered. "You're considered a genius."

"I'm considered a lot of things," he laughed. "A prick, a manipulator, a man-diva—and also someone who knows how to spot talent both behind and in front of the camera. You, my dear heart, have both."

"Me?"

"You. You not only saved a disastrous morning...look."

Charley clicked through the computer images. It was a series she hadn't seen before. Why? Because she was in them with Nikki.

Nikki was in khaki shorts and hiking boots, her rich black hair tied in a bandana. Charley was in the clothes she was still wearing, nearly identical to those for the shoot.

She was fresh faced, wearing no makeup since she wasn't supposed to be on camera, and her chestnut brown hair was flowing freely in the wind. They were under an umbrella tree with its rich green leaves and sandy bark, the bright blue of the African sky behind them. In the distance several vultures circled over a kill.

"Amazingly nice composition, Vince," she said.

"I know these weren't supposed to be 'real' shots. You were just illustrating the pose I wanted," he said pointedly. "But look at these, Charley. You've got 'it.' If nothing else comes from this entire job, I've made a discovery. You."

Charley was thrown. She was flattered. She was confused. "I'm your discovery?"

Vince chuckled.

"Why's that funny?" she asked.

"You're just so damned cute. You have an amazingly enigmatic expression on your face in these shots, Charley. One famously captured by DaVinci, captivating the world for years, but you don't see it when it's you."

"Yeah, right," she scoffed.

"So right, I'm going to call you Mona from now on," he said, gazing directly into her flecked hazel eyes.

The way he looked at her was captivating, too. There was a passion in what he said, a charisma she hadn't recognized before.

She laughed.

"And that smile is even better, 'Mona,'" he said pointedly.

She scoffed at the absurdity of it all.

"Lisa," she corrected him. "I think I like Lisa better."

"Now I am serious, you," he said as he pulled her up from the sofa. "Come here and look. If Brigitta's out of the picture, and she just may be, we always have you."

"What?" she reeled.

"This is business, Charley, and I've got to protect the shoot."

There was a massive carved teak mirror on the far side of the room. He led her there, with Charley resisting the whole way.

"Look!"

Charley looked at her reflection and was a bit shocked. She hadn't looked in a mirror all morning. The girl in that mirror was enigmatic, glowing, and beautiful in the most organic and natural way. In the peace and serenity of her African surroundings, she exuded an animal sexuality.

She smiled at the realization that he was right.

Then she caught him staring hungrily at her. Vince's hand slid quickly down her back, and he cupped her behind in his massive hand. Charley turned abruptly, and he began kissing her brusquely.

She was stunned as Vince wrapped his other strong arm around her and pulled her tightly to himself.

Charley pulled back, furious. But Vince was used to getting what he wanted.

"One other thing I am is an amazing lover," he said.

"You're all alike, aren't you?" she snarled. "Just like my father."

Her expression was no longer Mona Lisa, but instead a mixture of hurt and anger. "Take your hands off me now, Mr. Castle."

"Hard to get. I like that even better," Vince said, grabbing her and kissing her. She pulled away and slapped him fully across the face.

"I'll be in the suite," she said evenly as he reeled. "When you're ready to work again, you know where to find me."

Adrenaline pumping, she strode out of the lapa, forgetting the danger that surrounded them.

∞

Without thinking, she walked out to the path alone and took big, deep breaths, leaning against one of the guardrails put there for protection. Just then, three wildly chattering monkeys streaked across the grounds toward her, teeth bared and angry.

Before she knew what hit her, Charley was shoved out of the way as the screeching monkeys flew past her. A body landed on top of her and held her still.

Charley could hear the monkeys chattering as they ran through the camp. And suddenly, finally, the only noise was her heavy breathing and the body lifting off her.

"Are you okay?" she heard.

A masculine hand reached out to help, and when she looked up, she saw Brendan.

Her heart skipped a beat. "I'm—fine," she said, repeating the lie she'd told Tuma and Vince earlier.

"Then don't you ever walk alone out here again, do you hear me?" There was panic in his eyes and anger in his voice.

Charley was thrown by his vehement reaction. "I'm fine. Really. I am."

She took his hand, and he helped her to her feet. His hand was strong and the feel of his flesh strangely familiar. She could see he was breathing as heavily as she was.

"Are *you* okay?" she asked, truly concerned.

"Fine," he said curtly.

But clearly he wasn't.

"I won't be so careless again. I promise," she said gently.

She met his gaze, and he met hers. He brushed some dirt off her cheek and sighed.

"I—didn't mean to yell at you," he said apologetically.

"It's all right," she answered. "It's your job to make sure everyone's safe."

He shook his head sadly. "Yes, but…it's not just that. I lost my wife in a freak accident on a game drive a little over a year ago."

"I'm so sorry," Charley said. He gripped her hand a little bit tighter.

"And seeing you in danger…" his voice trailed off. "I usually don't talk about it," he admitted. "I don't know why I just did." He went silent. Numb.

Charley sensed he was reliving the moment when he had lost his wife. "I know about losing people you love…" She immediately pulled his face toward hers until their eyes locked.

In that split second, Charley understood love at first sight. Well, second or third sight. And it startled her.

"I should have been more careful. I'm sorry," she said softly. "Can we just pretend it never happened?"

He was lost in her eyes, her compassion, and her heart.

"Sure, we'll pretend that never happened," he said smiling. "As long as we never forget what just did."

∞

Charley's mind was a muddle as she and Brendan walked in silence through the maze of tree-lined paths that led back to the suite. Brendan slipped his arm around her slim waist, and she wrapped her arm through his. The fit was perfect, like two halves of a jagged heart necklace.

They reached the magnificent thatched residence, and Charley leaned against the door.

"Thank you," she said simply. "And I really am—"

He put his hand to her lips.

"I know, you're sorry." He stared at this girl he'd known less than twenty-four hours. "And I didn't mean to lay all that on you."

"I'm glad you did," she said.

Don't hate me for being happy that you're single, she grimaced to herself.

"I've managed to move on," he said.

Am I a creep for being glad I'm single? he thought to himself.

"Would you like to come in?" she asked, suddenly choking back the question and realizing how it sounded.

But Brendan didn't move his eyes from hers. "Would it be out of line for me to kiss you?" he said.

She shook her head no.

He moved in slowly. Their lips touched gently, fitting as though they were the negative and positive of the same print. There they lingered.

Charley turned the door handle behind her back. It clicked and opened. The tension was palpable.

"I would come in, but I can't," Brendan said as he pulled

away gently. "I've got something important I have to take care of this afternoon."

Charley felt her face flush. She had been willing to invite him into her room and maybe even into her bed. Was she being rejected?

"Oh, well, thanks again?" she said, realizing how hollow it sounded.

"You're welcome." He smiled. "Don't forget your promise to be careful," he reminded her as he walked away.

Charley watched the man with whom she had fallen head over heels stride down the path away from her.

"What just happened?" she said in disbelief. *And what could be more important than this?*

43  *ABBY AND CHELSEA*

CHELSEA WAS ON HER COMPUTER WHEN THE FRONT DOOR unlocked and Abby stormed in. She was near tears and furious with herself.

"How could I have been so stupid, Chels?" she wailed as she slammed the door behind her. "How could I have believed that ring would be on my hand forever?"

"Oh, Abs, I am so sorry," Chelsea offered.

"Jackson Gaines has his pick of the women in London, if not the world, and I thought he'd fallen in love with me. What was I thinking?"

Abby ripped off her coat and tossed it angrily.

"And what I put you through, just after you got dumped by that louse Max Brady. Me all smiles and giggles and dripping with love and enthusiasm while you were hurting. I'm obviously not only a lousy girlfriend, but also a lousy friend. Can you forgive me?"

Chelsea just stared at her best friend.

"I was afraid they might be including the ring," she said.

"Yep," Abby said, not really paying attention to Chelsea as she thrust her empty left hand in the air and then flipped her middle finger. "To you, Jackson Gaines."

"I'm confused, though. He broke up with you over that?"

"Yes! No ring. Empty finger. Broken heart."

"I don't believe it."

"Oh, you can believe it. We'd had a fabulous night in bed, celebrating, I thought…then he just said, 'I have to have the ring back.' Just like that."

"And then 'I'm breaking up with you'?" Chelsea questioned.

"He couldn't even get those words out of his mealy mouth. I told him exactly what I thought of him, what my *father* thought of him, and waved the no-good tool good-bye."

"And you're sure he was calling off the wedding?" Chelsea asked, tilting her head.

"What kind of question is that?" Abby snapped.

"There's something I think you should see. Radaronline?" Chelsea said, turning the computer screen toward her friend. "They scooped you, I think."

"I don't care about them today!" Abby said incredulously.

"It's about the upcoming auction," Chelsea said simply. "And you."

Abby reeled. "Wha—?"

On the screen was the radaronline.com website, Abby's biggest competition. The lead story had a photo of Abby and Chelsea from the day before, exiting the building in Wapping. The ring on Abby's left hand was circled, with a photo next to it of Olivia Gaines, Jackson's mother, wearing the spectacular yellow diamond. The headline read: To the Auction Block?

"Maybe if the paps hadn't gotten a shot of you wearing it yesterday, you could have kept it at least for a while."

"Oh, no…" Abby said as she read the gossip about Richie Gaines, the upcoming auction, and speculation that the ring would bring a pretty penny. "Anyone wanting to walk a mile in Olivia Marini Gaines' OMG shoes will have a chance to purchase them and hundreds of other personal items in the upcoming auction of the late fallen financier Richard Gaines' spoils next month. Sources say the four-carat yellow diamond, shown yesterday on the ring finger of Abigail Deveraux, won't be there long. Too bad her fiancé can't afford a new one!" Abby was sputtering now, and her eyes wide as saucers.

"So, Jackson never said 'I don't want to marry you,'" Chelsea said in a tone that made Abby's knees weak.

"No…" Abby admitted.

"And what did you say?" Chelsea asked.

Abby's face went white as everything began to sink in.

"Oh, Chelsea…what have I done?"

44 *MARLENA, PATCH, KAYLA, BILL, AND CORNELIUS*

BY THE TIME THE TOM-ALI VAN MADE IT BACK FROM MAPUSHA, the line outside the clinic had vanished. Patch attempted to drive into the parking lot carefully, but he hit a pothole. With the van's worn shocks and the gravel surface, the vehicle bounced badly.

"Ow! Ow! Ow!" Joe wailed from inside as he woke with a start.

"Sorry, Bud," Patch said, wincing at the pain he could only imagine Joe was feeling. The small dose of pediatric morphine that Kayla had given the boy was starting to wear off.

The door to the clinic opened, and Bill emerged as Patch scrambled from the driver's seat.

"What's going on?" Bill asked as he approached.

"Joe was a boy being a boy," Patch answered. "Thought he could fly."

"Broken arm?" Bill asked as they moved to the passenger's side.

"Wrist," Patch confirmed.

"Let me help you with him," Bill said as the door panel on the passenger's side slid open.

Joe was on Kayla's lap and whimpering again.

"Get Cornelius out here to help," Kayla insisted as she glared at Patch.

"He had to make a run to Londolani," Bill said. He was aware that Kayla was wary of him, even though he felt steady as a rock at the moment. "If you don't trust me, Beauty can give a hand."

"No," Kayla snapped. She was frazzled and angry with Joe, Steve, and Beauty—but mostly with herself. "And Cornelius was covering for me today! He shouldn't have left you here alone."

"I've got him," Patch said firmly. This was his son, and he was going to handle it.

Kayla glanced at Marlena, who nodded. "It was an accident," her friend reminded her.

"Come on, Sport," Patch said gently. "Let's get you inside."

Kayla gingerly inched Joe to the doorway. "Remember to keep that arm as still as you can."

Beauty scrambled inside the clinic to get a room ready.

∞

Marlena stayed in the waiting area with Bill while Kayla tended to Joe's injury.

"Kayla's upset with herself," she said gently.

"As Patch said, 'Boys'll be boys,'" Bill answered.

"That's not entirely it," Marlena clarified. "You know how much Kayla loves all of those villagers."

"And they love her."

"Well, one of the boys reached out to help Joe when he fell. They'd been playing, and the boy had some open cuts on his hands."

"Ah," Bill said, understanding.

"Her first thought was HIV, and she panicked," Marlena offered.

"I'd have thought the same," Bill admitted. "I obviously did."

"We all need to be kind to ourselves," she said. "All of us."

Bill knew she was talking about him, and he appreciated it.

"She was also annoyed with Cornelius because the van wasn't fully stocked. There were no splints or fiberglass to cast Joe."

Bill's heart sank. He knew that they were low on supplies because of his bad financial situation and that Cornelius opted to keep them in the clinic itself, not in the van.

"I think we could all use some compassion and maybe some iced tea," she added gently.

Bill nodded, appreciating her warmth.

Marlena took down glasses from the shelf as Bill retrieved the tea from the small fridge. Only four glasses were on the shelf, plus one nearly out of reach.

Bill retrieved his glass from the high shelf as Patch came from the exam room leading Joe by the hand. Joe's wrist was in a sling, supporting the bright yellow cast Kayla had fit so perfectly on him.

"Hey, pal," Bill said, smiling. "Look at you."

"This one's a tough little cookie," Kayla said with a sigh.

"Like his daddy, I bet," Marlena offered.

"Tough as nails," Patch said, giving Joe their special high-five with his opposite hand.

Joe tapped his daddy's hand and finally managed a smile.

As Patch kissed Joe on the top of his head, Kayla turned to Bill, who was relieved. They shared a look.

"I'm sorry for snapping at you out there, Bill," Kayla said apologetically.

"Can we drink to that?" he asked lightly.

"Sure," Kayla nodded, glancing at her husband and son.

The mood had shifted, and the warmth of their camaraderie had returned.

"Tea all around," Bill suggested.

"Let me help you," Marlena offered as Kayla and Patch comforted Joe.

Bill took a pitcher of brewed tea from the small fridge as Marlena retrieved the glasses from the open shelves, including the one with the gold "H."

"Tea for you, too?" Patch asked Joe.

The little boy nodded, and Marlena handed Patch a glass for the toddler and one for himself.

Kayla accepted hers from Bill, and they all raised their glasses.

"To friendship," she said with a smile.

"Amen," Bill agreed.

As they drank in silence, the door opened again and Cornelius entered, startled to see the assembly.

Having calmed down, Kayla gave him a half smile. "I forgive you, too, Cornelius."

"Great," he answered, wondering why. As she tipped her glass, he realized all of them were drinking tea and he noticed that the glass from the high shelf was missing. From the way they were holding the glasses he couldn't determine who had the glass with the "H." The glass that was dusted with powdered Rohypnol.

One of them got the roofie, he realized. *If there's a God, let it have been Bill.*

45  *JOHN, SCARLETT, AND JACKSON*

SCARLETT TOOK A LONG DRINK FROM A CUP OF BLACK COFFEE as she and John sat at one of the tables next to the pool.

"Thanks. I guess I needed this," she said as she lowered the cup from her lips.

"One cup's not enough to sober you up," he said pointedly.

"Do you really want me sober?" she asked flirtatiously.

"Want to tell me where all this is coming from?" John said.

Neither John nor Scarlett was aware that Charley had seen them together at the spa. If John had known, he'd have followed Charley.

"I'm a woman, you're a man—"

"And you're not looking to get laid, you're looking to be protected," he answered. "You were shaking like a leaf earlier. Want to tell me what's going on?"

"Maybe if you tell me what's going on with you two and Charley Gaines." Scarlett was nothing if not direct.

"Long story," John dodged.

"Mine, too," Scarlett answered. She glanced away, thinking

about the danger she'd stumbled into and the proposition she'd made to Cornelius.

"You're still shaking," John said as he attempted to get her to open up. He could almost feel her mind whirling.

"I'm cold," she lied, forcing a smile.

"In hundred-degree weather. I rather doubt that." He knew she was lying, but he knew not to push. "If you were going for a massage, you could have it in your suite. But I'm sure you know that."

"Or I could have it in yours. I heard your wife's out doing her good deeds for the day," she said as she batted her baby blues.

"If you're in some kind of danger, I'd like you to tell me. I've worked in various kinds of law enforcement, even been a cop. I might be able to help you."

The revelation made Scarlett's blood run cold. Or you might get me killed, she thought.

"Always did love a man in a uniform," Scarlett said glibly as she rose from her wicker chair.

As she stood, she stumbled but managed to catch herself.

"Right now, Miss O'Hara, you need to get some rest," John said firmly. "Let me have someone get you an escort."

As he moved into the spa, Scarlett's bravado slipped.

"Maybe a few hours in bed alone would do me some good," she said softly.

And I'll figure out how to get out of this mess I've gotten myself into.

∞

Uuka escorted Scarlett back to her suite. As she entered, she saw it was bustling once again. Ashley and the assistant were rapidly going through wardrobe with Nikki.

"Hey," Scarlett said. She was still a bit of a mess: barefoot, with a few scratches on her legs, and her hair drying naturally after her outdoor shower.

"Hey," Nikki answered.

"We're shooting on the game ride tonight and then in the Bedouin tent set up under the stars," Ashley informed her curtly. "Your wardrobe's here. Everyone's in cream. No discussion."

"Would you like me to try it on?" Scarlett asked.

"It'll be fine," Ashley said. "We'll see you later." Then she turned to Nikki and addressed her warmly. "Thanks for being such a professional."

Nikki nodded as they exited. Scarlett, though, was hurt. The production team was as cold to her as it was hot outside, and John's attempts to calm her vanished.

"If you'd have found those dead rhino, you'd have freaked, too." Scarlett spat.

"Jobs are hard to come by these days, and our reputations are all on the line. You know that. Brigitta's probably not going to be able to shoot again tonight so everyone's on edge," Nikki reminded her.

"Does anyone realize I'm the one with the most to lose?" Scarlett shouted. "I'm *thirty-nine*, for God's sake. Next year I'll be old enough for the cover of *MORE*!"

"I'm getting some beauty rest," Nikki said. She always tried to be nice, but even she was getting fed up with Scarlett. "Maybe you should, too."

Nikki strode out and closed the door, leaving Scarlett alone and more frustrated than ever.

"My life was also just threatened, dammit," she said, near tears. "Not that anyone cares…"

∽

The high-canopied bed looked luxurious with its Pratesi sheets, but it also looked lonelier than ever. Scarlett was truly scared. Sure, she'd stood up to Cornelius, and that was something. But she realized that if she said a word to anyone there, she could end up dead. When Cornelius had spoken to her, she'd realized he had the eyes of a killer.

Why didn't I tell John Black? she thought to herself.

Her hand went to her right eye.

Because I want that rhino horn for myself, she admitted.

She tried to calm herself by taking deep breaths, but that didn't work. She tried meditation next, but that lasted for less than sixty seconds.

When all else fails…the hair of the dog, she thought wryly.

She took the two remaining miniature bottles of vodka from the minibar and drank them straight. As she shook off the potent aftertaste, the phone at her bedside table rang, startling her.

Who wants to land on me now? she wondered.

She looked at the phone and contemplated not answering.

Maybe Cornelius?

Finally, she couldn't take the ringing anymore so she answered. Her eyes lit up when she heard Jackson's voice.

"You don't know how much I needed this right now, baby," she slurred. "How are you?"

"Things have been better," Jackson admitted. He was calling from Chance's loft in Soho. "In other words, life right now is shit."

"I hear you, lover."

"Aside from not being able to get work since it hit the fan last summer and my flat heading for the auction block, my fiancée thinks I broke up with her because of you."

Scarlett sat back, taking it all in.

"Your flat's going on the auction block?" she asked through her haze.

"I'm calling to ask you to tell her it isn't true."

"I need you, Jackson."

"Aren't you listening to me?" he snapped.

"Not that way," she answered with a soggy lilt in her voice. "We were good together. And now I have a way we can both make oodles of money. Not exactly Richie Gaines kind of money but major cash, and I know if there's anyone I can trust with my life it's you."

"What the hell are you talking about?" Jackson was more frustrated than ever. But as a financial pariah, he was willing to listen to any idea about making money.

Jackson sat stunned as Scarlett told him about her encounter with Cornelius. She refused to reveal the poacher's name, but she assured Jackson she knew this was the real deal because she'd overheard the exporters discussing it.

"How do I fit in?" he asked.

Scarlett reminded her ex that he'd run his father's financial empire, not to mention overseeing his mother's hugely successful OMG fashion house. In other words, he had talent and moneyed contacts galore.

"Isn't that killing an endangered species?" Jackson asked with a tone of disbelief.

Chance reeled as he overheard.

"If I back out, I'm the one who's endangered," Scarlett said. "Besides, it is so common here. Think of it like Big Game hunting, only better. Instead of a trophy for your wall, you'll get buckets of money, money, money."

There was silence on the phone.

"Can I count on you, Jackson?" she asked softly.

There was a longer silence. "Can I count on you to talk to Abby?" he finally asked in return.

When the call was over, Jackson sat in stunned silence.

"What was that all about?" Chance asked as he poured his brother a shot of tequila and handed it to him.

"Scarlett and some unbelievably dangerous scheme she stumbled on," Jackson admitted.

"Endangered species?" Chance said incredulously.

"Rhino," Jackson nodded, his expression sobering. "We never should have let Charley go down there."

46  MARLENA, JOHN, AND BILL

DRESSED IN LIGHTWEIGHT KHAKIS AND AN OPEN SHIRT, John felt the breeze as he opened the door for room service. Marlena would be back soon, and if he knew his "Doc" well, she'd be famished. He waved the waiter inside.

The African waiter placed the ebony wood tray on the table nearest the lounge chair, the one with the best view of the wonderment that was Africa. Under the silver domes were beautiful shrimp cocktails and an assortment of local fruits and breads. A bottle of champagne rested nearby in an ice bucket.

John tipped the waiter, who bowed and exited on cat feet, and then made sure bubble bath and oils were ready near the claw-foot tub.

"You deserve to be pampered, Doc," he said. "The best for my best."

The sound of vultures cawing in the distance caught his attention. He moved to the deck and looked into the vastness.

"What's in the air today?" he asked himself rhetorically.

He heard footsteps from the walkway approaching the suite.

Excited, he popped open the champagne. He heard the door open and turned back toward it to greet his wife. And stopped cold.

Marlena stumbled into the room, escorted by Bill Horton.

"Hiiiii…" Marlena giggled as she moved out of Bill's arms.

"Well, hello," John said as he gave Bill a quizzical look.

Marlena was clearly tipsy, which John hadn't expected.

"It went well today, I guess," John said as Marlena smiled broadly.

"Joe broke his arm," she slurred. "He thought he could fly," she added, extending her arms.

"Okay, maybe not so well," John said. "So you guys were celebrating what then?"

"What—?" Marlena asked. "My, am I exhausted. You would have loved it, John," she rambled. "The women create these gorgeous tapestries, all to help each other survive. I'd forgotten how beautiful they are. Amazing. Just soooo amazing."

She was getting drowsier by the minute. Her head dipped as she tried to shake off her fogginess. "Is that champagne?" she asked, seeing the bottle. "I am thirst-y."

"I think you may have had enough, Doc," John said gently.

"Enough?" she said. "We haven't had any," she said as she walked over to the table.

She raised a glass in a toast. "To the most wonderful man in the world—and to my husband," she said, looking between Bill and John. She was giddier than John had seen her in ages.

When she'd finished the glass, she set it on the nearby table and sank into the large comfy chair.

"Sure…you haven't had any alcohol today," John said, giving her a look of disbelief.

She shook her head slowly.

"Actually, we haven't," Bill told him. He was as confused as John. "I know they didn't have any while they were working, and at the clinic all we had was iced tea."

Marlena was beginning to doze off. The champagne she had just added to her system would only amplify the effect of the drug she'd unknowingly ingested.

"I think I'd better get her into bed," John said.

"Maybe I should help you," Bill said, pointing at Marlena, now sound asleep and dead weight in the chair.

"I've got it, but thanks," John answered. "When did she start acting all...like that?" he said, swirling his hands around his head.

"About halfway over here she started to get spacey," Bill told him. "Really out of character for her. I guess there's a lot of that going around lately," he added, thinking about himself.

"Well, thanks for bringing her back," John said with a tone that Bill knew meant John was asking him to leave.

"'Welcome," Bill said. "Maybe I'll see you tomorrow."

"Maybe," John answered, his thoughts only on his inebriated wife.

Bill headed for the door as John swept Marlena up in his arms and carried her to the bed.

At the door, Bill stopped and looked back. Well...not exactly the time to ask a man for a barrel of money, he said to himself, and he slowly exited.

John tenderly took off Marlena's shoes and placed her in a comfortable sleeping position. She was out like a light. "Are you okay, baby?" he asked as he brushed the hair from her forehead.

The phone rang and she stirred slightly. He picked it up quickly to keep from waking her.

"John Black here," he answered.

"John, it's Jackson Gaines. I'm here with Chance, and you're the only one who can help us."

47  *PATCH AND KAYLA*

THE DRIVE FROM TOM-ALI TO STEVE AND KAYLA'S HOME wasn't long, but it was a tense one. Kayla's jaw was set as she held Joe on her lap. While she knew having him ride without a seatbelt was dangerous, she needed to comfort the little boy who had discovered he couldn't really fly.

Every time the Jeep hit a bump, Joe whimpered in pain. They were reminded of just how primitive the roads were with every jostle.

When the Jeep stopped, Joe rested his head against Kayla's chest. The stillness and her warmth were a comfort.

"Wait in Mommy's arms until I come and get you," Steve said.

"I want her to carry me," Joe answered. He wouldn't look at his dad. After Kayla's outburst at Mapusha, Joe was convinced this wasn't his fault but his father's.

"We all make mistakes, Joe," Steve said calmly. "Sometimes they're just a little more painful."

Joe didn't respond, and Kayla was distant. "Could you open the door, please?" she asked with a tone stripped of emotion.

"Sure thing," Steve answered.

SHERI ANDERSON

He climbed out of the driver's side and went around to open the door for Kayla.

"The cast won't be completely set for another few hours, so you need to keep the sling on. Okay, sweetie?" Kayla asked gently.

Joe nodded.

Kayla tried to get out of the car with Joe on her lap, but that was impossible. So Patch gingerly hoisted his son to the ground. Movement was still painful, though, and Joe yelped.

"Mommy!"

Kayla slipped out of the front seat, taking Joe's good arm and guiding her frightened son away from Patch and into the house.

∞

Joe had been up all day without a proper nap and was exhausted from his experience. Kayla took him into his room without speaking to her husband. She was still a jumble of emotions.

Steve took an icy mug and a chilled wineglass out of the freezer, and poured them each a libation.

After a while, Kayla appeared from Joe's room. Steve handed her a glass of her favorite white.

"You've gotta forgive me at some point, Sweetness," Steve said. "I thought Beauty had it covered."

"I know…I do," she said as she took the glass. She found it hard to stay mad at him for long. "But you understand why I have to fire her and do not want her caring for Joe."

"Yeah, unfortunately I do," he answered. "She's a great kid, but you have to have people you can totally trust."

Kayla took a sip of her wine, and her eyes met his. "I let myself down with those awful thoughts I had when that boy was trying to help Joe. And then Cornelius let me down in a huge way. Not having the van totally stocked is unforgivable."

She was adamant, and Steve felt a twinge of guilt.

"I'm sure he had his reasons."

"Like what?" Kayla snapped. "He'd known for two days that we were going out there…"

"Come on, Kayla, give the guy a break."

"Our son had to travel over ridiculously bumpy roads while trying to keep his wrist together. Doesn't that make you angry?"

"It does, but—"

"But what, Steve?" she said, cutting him off.

Kayla knew Steve well. He had the same look on his face that she'd noticed after he'd seen Bill the other day. He looked her squarely in the eye but said nothing.

Kayla set her glass down with such force that it nearly shattered. "Something's going on, and you're going to tell me!"

Steve stepped back in shock. "Okay, there is…But I promised Bill I'd give him a few days before I said anything," Steve said. "I'm a man of my word, Sweetness."

"You gave me your word you'd never lie to me," she insisted.

"I haven't lied," Steve implored.

"If this is something I should know, it's a lie of omission!"

Steve looked at her long and hard. He knew Kayla was right, and the last thing he ever wanted was to lie to her. He took a deep sigh.

"The money for the clinic is gone. Bill invested it with some creep who ended up being another Madoff. That's why the extra supplies have been low—"

"And none of the repairs have been done," she said aghast, finishing his sentence. Her eyes widened. "The new van?"

"Not gonna happen without a miracle."

"When did you know that?" she asked, glaring at him.

"When I went over to his place," Steve said, trying to defend himself. "The poor guy said he just needed a few weeks to get things in order."

"A few weeks!" Kayla was horrified. "And when were you going to tell me all this, Steven?"

"Kayla, calm down."

"I will not! We can't stop providing services for these people. It's life or death for some of them, for God's sake." She began to unspool. "Do we even have enough for the people who will show up tomorrow?"

She went and grabbed her purse from the entry table.

"What are you doing?"

"I'm going back there."

"Now?"

"No, in a month when the place is shuttered," she said sarcastically. "And since we have no one to watch Joe, it'll have to be you. If I can trust you."

She pulled the keys from her handbag and stormed out, slamming the door behind her.

"Well, that didn't go well," Steve said as he stared at the closed door.

The room felt emptier than ever. He and Kayla rarely had arguments in their marriage, much less a fight. And he knew her hurt and anger were warranted.

"Mommy?" Steve heard from the hallway, the sound breaking his reverie.

The noise has awakened Joe.

"Where's Mommy?" Joe asked meekly as he entered from his room.

"She'll be back soon, Bud," Steve promised. "I'm sorry about all this. You know that, don't you?"

Joe nodded slightly. Then his face screwed up and he began to sob. Over his son's wailing, Steve heard Kayla's Jeep tear out of the driveway.

So much for the serenity of Africa, Steve thought dryly as he went to comfort Joe.

48  *JOHN AND THE ISA*

"Rhino poaching," John said under his breath as he entered the Londolani library. The plantation-shuttered room also served as the facility's gift shop and business center.

None of the suites had wireless reception, and while John had brought his laptop with him, it was basically useless and he wanted to access the ISA computer bank in London now.

Besides, Marlena was out cold.

John's mind was nothing if not analytical, and he weighed Jackson's call carefully. Scarlett involved with rhino poachers? Was it actually true? Or was the desperate and drunk girl who had come on to him at the spa just screaming to her ex-boyfriend for attention?

If it was reality, someone at the game farm had to be involved because Scarlett and the others had only left the property together. And if it was someone at the game farm, any and all of them were in danger.

There was a Mac on one of the highly polished dark wood desks. John had learned much earlier that the best way to be inconspicuous was to hide in plain sight. So he slid onto the chair in front of the computer and logged on.

When he entered www.isa.int, the website for the International Security Alliance immediately appeared on the screen. He entered his user name and password but got the prompt "User Name or Password Incorrect." After several attempts, he discovered his clearance had been blocked.

Trying another strategy, he typed the words "Rhino Poaching South Africa" into Google.

Within a nanosecond, dozens of articles appeared. While Brendan had made them all aware of the situation, John had had no idea of the depth and magnitude of the rampant slaughtering.

The demand for rhino horn had exploded. In the last year, it had escalated 3000 percent. The most recent article detailed the arrest of the eleven alleged poachers on New Year's Day. The photo accompanying the report had been shot on the steps of the Johannesburg Central Police Station, which had once been the nerve center of apartheid repression.

Most of the eleven were well-dressed Caucasians with heads down and arms handcuffed behind them. A crowd watched as they were being escorted into the nondescript blue-and-white building.

John clicked on another story, equally disturbing, from several months earlier in which a half dozen others had been arrested for poaching. Again, a crowd watched as the men were being incarcerated.

John studied the photos for any clues they could offer. He paused at the sight of a striking Asian woman who appeared in each of the crowds.

Using a facial recognition application, he clicked on all of the images he felt were similar, and the software informed him that they were indeed a match. When he zoomed in on the grainy photos, he was startled to realize he knew the woman.

"Jiao-jie?" he gasped.

"Yes?" he heard from several feet away.

He turned to see that Jiao-jie and Wen were standing no more than ten feet away at the glass-encased jewelry display on the gift-shop counter.

"I thought I heard your voice." John smiled as he calmly shut down the computer.

"We were going to ask Mr. Castle if he would like to use any of these in his shoot tonight," Wen said, smiling. From the tone in Wen's voice and his demeanor, John was certain they weren't aware of what he'd discovered.

"They are beautiful," John said.

"These would be especially lovely on your wife," Jiao-jie said as she pointed to a pair of dazzling blue-diamond earrings she'd been admiring.

John took a look at the price and let out a whistle.

"Is that 1,600,000?"

"Rand," Wen nodded. "Roughly 230,000 U.S. dollars."

"We know you're a man of taste and money," Jiao-jie said with a smile.

Do they also know I'm former ISA? John wondered.

"And my wife would love these," he admitted. "But that's a little rich for her blood. And mine."

"We've all got to make money somehow," Wen said with a wink.

Yeah, and how are you doing it? John thought.

"Will we see you both at dinner?" Jiao-jie asked as she placed the diamonds back in the case.

"Not sure," John admitted. "Marlena's pretty exhausted."

"Well, we hope to," Jiao-jie added. "We have to check stock at our other venders so we won't be on the game ride, but it would be lovely to see her again before we leave in the morning. She's so charming and funny."

"In case we miss you, do you have a card?" John asked.

"Absolutely," Wen said as he took a card from his wallet.

"Thanks, Jiao-jie and Wen Xing," John said as he read the card.

"Now you won't forget us," Jiao-jie said, smiling.

"Oh, don't worry," he assured them. "That's definitely not going to happen."

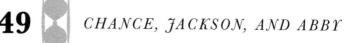
"NEARLY A MILLION DOLLARS ON THE BLACK MARKET?" Chance said to Jackson, who was now on his second tequila.

"That's what Scarlett said."

"Drunk."

"And she thinks we have the connections to help her sell it," Jackson said incredulously.

"After Elle Macpherson took that heat for saying she took it, does Scarlett think anyone would touch it?" Chance asked.

"Is that true?" Jackson said, answering the question with a question.

"She denied it later in the press, but from what I hear in 'the underground,' yep, she's been taking it for years."

"And 'your' underground would probably know," Jackson said, agreeing.

Chance was considered one of the hottest of the hot in the international gay community. Or he had been until his father had stripped a lot of them of their hard-earned cash.

"Sick, really," Chance said shuddering. "The idea of blowing rhinos away and sawing off those horns."

"Really?"

Chance looked at his brother quizzically.

"What're those?" Jackson said indicating a trio of shiny cream-colored balls that sat in a shiny Nambé metal bowl on Chance's mantel.

"Ivory, why?" Chance asked.

"From?"

"One of Dad's ex-lawyers who was gay and gave me the balls because he wanted mine," Chance answered. "Tacky guy, really."

"Are they real? Maybe real African elephant ivory?" Jackson asked. "From slaughtered elephants?"

Chance reeled. "I actually don't know."

"And what if their carcasses were left to rot or be eaten by scavengers?"

"I get the point. But I already agree we shouldn't do this." Chance was appalled.

"I'm just saying maybe it's time we took a good look at ourselves and our priorities. Rhino horn, ivory, diamonds. Shiny beautiful objects that we've paid fortunes for without ever thinking about the blood, sweat, and tears that have been shed for them."

"Wow," Chance said.

"I mean it, bruv," Jackson said anxiously. "Our parents screwed up our priorities, and maybe it's time we paid back. So who cares if we lose the flats and the cars and the diamonds?" Jackson pulled the dazzling yellow sparkler from his pants pocket. "They're just things!"

There was a loud knock on the front door.

"Come in!" Jackson shouted.

"Well, it's actually my place," Chance said as he made his way across the parquet floor. "But whoever it is can come in, I suppose."

Jackson turned the ring over in his fingers as his brother opened the front door.

It was Abby.

The look between her and Chance said volumes. He nodded in the direction of his brother.

"Why don't I get us something to take the chill off," Chance said, making a hasty retreat. He turned on his heel and exited toward the kitchen backwards. "You two. Talk."

"I heard about the auction," she said with an apologetic tone.

"I figured you would," he said, shifting uncomfortably. "I'm sorry you've been dragged into it."

"And you weren't calling off the engagement, were you," she said as a statement more than a question.

He simply shook his head no.

"What can I say?" Abby grimaced, mortified. "I've already said way, way, way too much."

"I don't have a job. Pretty soon I won't have a flat, and I definitely don't have a ring, so how can I ask you to still marry me?"

There was an agonizing silence.

"Just say 'marry me.'" she said simply. "Please…!"

"I don't have a job. Pretty soon I won't—" he repeated.

"Marry me!" she said cutting him off as tears formed in her eyes. "If you can't say it, I will. Jackson Gaines, will *you* marry *me*?"

There was a long silence, as Jackson took it all in. This beautiful girl was standing in front of him, knowing he would always carry the scent of his father's misdeeds. Yet she still wanted to marry him?

Abby hadn't taken a breath for what seemed like hours. As she gazed at him with dewy eyes, the reality of her love washed over him. And as if the weight of the world had been lifted off his shoulders, Jackson broke into a slow grin.

"Do you have any idea what you're really getting yourself into?"

"Yes!"

Elated, Abby jumped into his arms and wrapped her legs around his waist.

"I love you, Jackson Gaines!"

She began covering him with kisses that grew longer and stronger. Their passion taking over, Jackson walked her to the sofa and laid her gently on her back.

"Ahem," they heard as Chance entered with a tray of steaming cocoa. "This is my place, remember?"

Jackson rolled off Abby, and now all he could do was laugh. "You're right, it's yours, bruv."

"Well, not mine for long," Chance grimaced, adding, "unless there's a miracle."

50 *CHARLEY, SCARLETT, AND CORNELIUS*

CHARLEY KNEW THE IMPORTANCE OF BEING IN TOP FORM for a shoot, so she did her best to get several hours of midday sleep. But her best wasn't good enough, and she stirred in bed.

From the debacle at the watering hole to her saving the day for Vince, to him forcing himself on her, to the run-in with the monkeys, and then to her over-the-moon, amazing connection with Brendan, the events of the day had her mind racing. But what was most on her mind was her mother.

Olivia Gaines had always been her best friend and confidant. Right now, Charley ached to have Olivia wanting every delicious detail of her falling in love for the first time.

Love, Charley thought. Her body shuddered as her hand went to her lips. *How can I love someone I just met, Mummy?*

Her gaze landed on the family album that sat next to the cut crystal lamp on the side table.

And can I love Marlena? she wondered. Is that disrespecting you?

There was a rap on her door.

"Hey, sunshine, we've got to get a move on." It was Vince. "Makeup call's in five minutes."

She realized she had lost track of the time.

"Sorry," she called out as she scrambled off the bed and hastily wrapped a light cotton robe around her slim body.

"I'm the one who's sorry, kiddo. Sorry about before," Vince said as she opened the door.

"I hear that," she said simply.

"I'm pretty used to getting my way with women. Well, with anyone I can get pretty much what I want. I appreciate you putting me in my place, actually. It says a lot about your character. You'll go far."

Charley shifted on her feet. "The slap was a little heavy," she said apologetically.

"It didn't do much damage," he offered. "Unfortunately, I can't say the same for Brigitta's fall. According to the gang, her face has swelled up like a purple and green balloon. So…"

"So—?" Charley asked.

"You're on, darlin'" Vince winked.

Charley immediately understood what he meant. She'd be in front of that camera.

"That's what happens when you've got 'it,'" he said, smiling.

∞

Being in a makeup chair wasn't unfamiliar for Charley. From the time she was three, Olivia had orchestrated every Gaines family portrait, during which Charley was treated like a Dresden doll.

Her parents had also dragged her and her brothers to the major

OMG fashion events around the world, where Charley had had to project the perfect image.

But she hated it then and wasn't crazy about it now.

The trouble was that her face was indeed the perfect canvas. Her skin was flawless and her features perfectly proportioned. Her wide eyes were accented by clean, arched eyebrows. Her lips pouted just so, and her slightly chiseled cheekbones welcomed a dusting of color.

The suite was buzzing with activity. Scarlett and Nikki were getting their hair done, while Brigitta sat on one of the plush sofas, holding an ice pack on her cheek as she fought back soft tears.

"Breathtaking," Greg said as he put the finishing touches on Charley. The rich ochre eye shadow picked up the hazel flecks in her smiling blue eyes. "And you have this, I don't know, glow I never noticed before."

Because it wasn't there before, she thought. Not until Brendan.

"What were you and Vince doing all afternoon, Charley?" Scarlett piped in. "I had that glow with him more than once, too."

Which is why he doesn't respect you, Scarlett, Charley thought. Instead she bit her tongue.

"And what were you up to this afternoon?" she asked pointedly. *Seducing John Black?* "Did you have some secret tryst, perhaps?"

Before Scarlett could reply, the ringing of the phone broke the moment. Nikki was closest and answered.

"She is here. Who can I say is calling? Okay, I'll get her."

"Scarlett," she said as she handed over the phone, "it's Cornelius from Tom-Ali Clinic for you."

Scarlett stiffened. But she managed to put on a coy smile as she got out of the stylist's chair and moved away for privacy.

"So, this is a surprise," she said into the phone.

"Just checking to make sure things are moving forward," Cornelius said. He was on a pay phone at the bar at Ambri, nursing a beer and looking out across the grassy plains as he spoke. "And let me hear how good you are at lying."

"Yes, I'm being a good girl, Cornelius. Took my malaria tablets exactly on time."

"Nice," he smiled. "Have you made any calls?"

"I did!" she said, being as evasive as she could under the circumstances. "Why would I lie to you?"

"Scarlett, come on," Alex said as he indicated with his hairbrush for her to get back in his chair.

"Hope I see you before we leave for Cape Town, too," Scarlett said into the phone. The others didn't see the fear creeping onto her thirty-nine-year-old face as she hung up.

"What can I say..." she shrugged. "He likes me."

Likes my connections, she said to herself. Because we're going to make a fortune. If he lets me live, that is...

∞

Buffalo could be seen emerging from the plains outside the bar as Cornelius drained the Carling Black Label from his tall glass. The late-afternoon crowd was filtering in. One of the rangers he'd conversed with when he and Patch were there with Bill slid onto the bar stool next to him.

"The usual?" the bartender asked.

"And one for my friend," the pleasant ranger said, smiling.

As the bartender went to the fridge for the beer, Cornelius

turned to him. "Tonight's going to be my last, Neil."

"I've heard that one before," Neil laughed. Like so many others, they had both been swept into the illegal trade that had become rampant.

"I'm serious," Cornelius said as he fiddled nervously with his empty glass. "Jiao-jie and Wen take off in the morning, and that's the last I'm dealing with them."

"Meaning?" Neil said, cocking his head.

"I owe them one last horn, and then I'm history. That arrest on New Year's Eve freaked me out. There's too much heat, and I've earned enough," he lied.

"So our connection to the Xings is over," Neil said as the bartender returned with the heady libations.

"Through me, yes," Cornelius answered. "Sorry, I just can't in good conscience do this anymore."

Neil ran his finger around the rim of his frosty glass as the news sank in.

"It is a pretty nasty business. I've been thinking of quitting for a while, too," he admitted.

"Really?" Cornelius said, startled.

"It's blood money is what it is. I guess fate's taking the decision out of my hands."

"We're doing the right thing," Cornelius said, pretending to reassure his friend.

"Yeah," Neil said as he started to choke up. "Thanks."

"You're doing the right thing," Cornelius repeated.

Because then there's all the more out there for me.

51  *KAYLA AND CORNELIUS*

A SQUEAL EMANATED FROM THE AIR CONDITIONER AT Tom-Ali as Kayla pored over the notes she'd been scribbling.

"Upgraded lab equipment, new autoclave, flooring we can sterilize properly," she sighed as she ticked items off her list. "That's just the tip of the iceberg."

She sank back in her chair and wiped her glistening brow. "Let's not forget new refrigeration."

She moved to the rattling cooler and banged it with her fist. "Bill promised this year we'd have new everything, and now if Steve's right, we can't even pay the electric bill. On top of all that, I'm talking to myself," she added ruefully. "Maybe I'm going mad," she said more loudly. "No, I am mad. Mad as hell!"

She began stamping her feet, screaming, and waving her arms wildly until she was exhausted.

Better, she said to herself as she ended her outburst. If anyone from Salem knew I do that to get it all out, they'd think I'm crazy.

Then as she caught her breath, she slowly sobered. *Am I crazy for putting my family in danger?*

She glanced out the clinic window and realized the sun was getting low in the sky. Villagers on rickety bikes and in minibuses were heading out of Hoedspruit. She checked her watch and blanched.

"I've been here over two hours?"

Kayla organized her notes quickly, went to the back rooms, and turned out the lights. As she returned to the waiting room, the phone was ringing.

She reached for the receiver but instead opted to let the answering system pick up. In a moment she heard over the speaker, "It's Steve just checking to make sure you'll be home before dark. Give me a call back. All's good here, Sweetness," he said. "For the record, I am sorry. And by the way, we love you."

Kayla stared at the phone and smiled softly. "Me, too. But I'd rather tell you in person."

Her purse and keys were by the door. She picked them up, shut off the lights, and exited.

From outside, she locked the door behind her. Neighboring small businesses were shutting down, and she nodded to their owners pleasantly as she got into the Jeep for the ride back to her family.

Moments after her Jeep disappeared down the dusty highway, Cornelius' truck pulled up to the side of the building.

∞

Cornelius flipped on the lights as he entered.

Now that the place was empty, his mission was simple.

He retrieved a pair of latex surgical gloves from one of the cabinet drawers and then went to the storage room and retrieved Bill's Browning A-Bolt from the locked cabinet.

Setting the rifle on the counter, he unlocked the meds cabinet and perused his options.

"Prescription courage, baby," he said as he took out a bottle of Adderall XR. He swallowed two of the amphetamine pills. They had been his friends since he'd gotten hooked in vet med school. He put a dozen or so in his pocket.

The next bottle out of the cabinet was Rohypnol. Another drug he knew all too well but for very different reasons.

Taking one of the clean drinking glasses from next to the sink, he used the base of it to crush several Rohypnol tablets. Then he rubbed the powdery substance between his thumb and forefinger sending a light dusting of the potent hypnotic into the glass.

He was just placing the spiked glass on the high shelf when the front door opened.

It was Kayla.

"Cannot believe I left the lights on…" she muttered under her breath as she entered. Then she stopped short as she saw Cornelius.

"Cornelius," she gasped.

"Hi," he said evenly, trying to act as nonchalant as possible.

Kayla knew she was in danger. It was impossible to ignore the gun, the gloves, and the drugs.

"I just came back to pick up my notes," she said quickly, looking away and indicating the tablet on the desk.

"Only one thing I can say about that, Kayla," he said as he moved toward her, pulling off the gloves. "Really bad timing."

"I didn't see anything," she gasped, holding up her hand to shield the view of the gun.

"And you're a very bad liar," he snapped. He was getting amped as the Adderall kicked in. "Oh, you saw something," he said. "But trust me, you won't remember it."

Before Kayla knew what had hit her, Cornelius had catapulted himself toward her, knocking her against the door. She hit the door hard and had the wind knocked out of her.

Her eyes met his as he grabbed her. "Sorry about this. Really," he said as he whirled her around and shoved her to the floor.

"Why?" she moaned as she lay there. Her eyes fluttered as she tried to shake off her disorientation and gasped for air.

Cornelius sprung to the counter where the remainder of the powdered Rohypnol sat and dumped it in a glass, diluting it with water.

Keeping an eye on his disoriented victim, he quickly retrieved a syringe. Then he filled it with the powerful sedative and returned, injecting it into her arm.

Kayla winced as the needle pierced her flesh.

Cornelius waited while the powerful sedative spread through her bloodstream, and within a minute, she was out cold.

He snapped his fingers in front of her several times and shook her lightly at first and then with more intensity. When he was sure she was under, he let out a huge sigh of relief.

Glancing around quickly, he noticed one of their medical kits next to the door. He tipped it over next to her feet and then positioned her limp body carefully to look as if she'd fallen over it and hit her face when she hit the ground.

"You should be more careful," he chided her. "Look what not paying attention got you."

Pleased with himself, Cornelius smiled. He knew that with the amount of the amnesiac he'd injected directly into her bloodstream, she'd never remember what she'd seen.

THE SUN WAS GOING DOWN IN THE TIMBAVATI AND SOFT LIGHT filtered through the trees into John and Marlena's suite. Her head rested in exactly the same position where John had put it nearly three hours ago.

"Doc," John said quietly as he pushed the hair back from her peaceful face. "How tired were you?"

He kissed the tip of her nose just as the bedside phone rang. Marlena repositioned herself slightly as John quickly answered.

"Shane?" It was indeed Shane Donovan, one of John's best friends and still a high-ranking agent in the ISA.

"I've been trying to reach you for hours." John was frustrated, and that was obvious in his voice.

"I just saw your messages," Shane answered apologetically. "I'm not quite awake, my friend."

John glanced at his sleeping wife. "Is there some sleeping epidemic I don't know about?"

"It's not even 8:00 a.m. in L.A.," Shane answered. "Besides, I left you two messages on your cell phone."

John took his iPhone from his pocket.

"I can only get spotty service here out in the middle of nowhere," John realized. "When I first heard about the poaching down here, it didn't make sense that it was so out of control. But the area's huge and communication ain't easy. I'm beginning to get it now. What are you doing in L.A.?"

"I'm here over the holiday…trying to work on things with Kim," Shane admitted.

Shane Donovan and Kim Brady Donovan were two of John's closest friends, and their relationship had been as much of a roller-coaster ride as John and Marlena's. The danger and uncertainty of being an international agent had taken its toll on so many. Kim and Shane's marriage had been one of the victims. Now Shane was juggling his position in London with trips to Los Angeles in hopes he could heal their scarred relationship.

"Glad to hear that," John said sincerely. "I know most of the problems were because of the ISA, and family's got to come first. But I need you desperately at the moment, pal."

"She's meeting me here at the hotel to talk in less than an hour. Yes, I am in a hotel. The Sunset Tower so I'm not complaining, but we're still on a rocky road," Shane said as he glanced out the window of the landmark Art Deco hotel with its panoramic view of greater Los Angeles. "I guess if anyone knows the hell of losing the love of your life you do."

John glanced at Marlena, who was beginning to stir. "I also know that when we see a wrong we have to right it," John said. "The slaughtering of rhino is still crippling this country."

"One would have thought Selebi's conviction would have made an impact," Shane offered.

The South African High Court had found Jackie Selebi, National Police Commissioner of South Africa, guilty for taking bribes from drug traffickers less than a year earlier. Also the former president of Interpol, Selebi had resigned from both posts and was on "extended leave."

"Just goes to show how high the corruption here goes," John said, disgusted. "Obviously why I'm keeping this close to the vest. We all believe in signs, Shane, and I landed in the heart of this for a reason. I tried to get into the ISA computers myself but I've lost my clearance."

"I'm all yours," Shane said simply.

"I need you to check on an Asian couple for me. Jiao-jie and Wen Xing. They're importers, but I think I know what they're exporting."

"Any chance you can spell those names for me?"

"As a matter of fact, I can."

John retrieved the business card he'd gotten from the couple and spelled the names for Shane. He began to pace as he spoke, his adrenaline pumping.

"They've got their own private jet on the airstrip here. A Falcon 200," he added.

"Isn't that what you owned?" Shane asked.

"Yep," John answered. "And if I'm right about this, I need one more little favor. I need you to break its emergency security code for me. Mine was registered with the builder of the aircraft. Dassault. Surely you can hack into their system for me."

"I'm sure I can," Shane assured him.

"Think you can get it done before you order breakfast?"

"I'll do my best," Shane repeated. "Right now, all you can do is wait."

"Wait by this friggin' phone." John's voice was filled with frustration.

"And this is the only number where I can reach you," Shane said as a statement more than a question.

"Guess they don't think you need good cell service in paradise."

"Stay cool," Shane reminded him.

"I know the drill. But I'm like a caged animal here, Donovan," John said pointedly. "And time is of the essence."

"I hear you. In our line of work, isn't it always?"

John hung up the phone, but he couldn't stop pacing.

"Hey," he heard softly.

Marlena was finally opening her eyes.

"Hi, Doc," John said as he entered the bedroom and quickly moved to her side. "You were really out of it."

"I still am a bit," she admitted as she yawned. "I didn't realize what an emotional day it would be."

"Me, too," John said with his own meaning.

"How did I get back here?"

Marlena's mind was fuzzy, exactly the side effect Cornelius had counted on to keep Bill's mind a muddle.

"Bill brought you."

"He did? I didn't realize I was so loopy."

Outside, she could see that the streaks of coral and purple in the sky were fading.

"Did we miss the game ride?" she asked.

"Do you still want to go?" he answered.

"Well…would you hate me if I just rested a while longer?"

"I can keep myself busy," he answered. "Why don't you sleep some more and we'll have a late dinner here."

"I love you," she said.

He tenderly kissed her. "You might want to get comfortable."

"I'm fine," she said drowsily. Her eyes were still heavy from the Rohypnol, and she began to drift back to sleep.

John moved from the bed and took the phone receiver out to the deck to wait for Shane's call. The stars were emerging like a blanket of twinkle lights laid across a heavenly garden. In the distance John could see a loping herd of impala, and he could hear the trumpet of an elephant.

It was now fully night. The animals were stirring. And soon, at the hands of mercenary men and women, some of them would be dying.

53  *CHARLEY*

THROUGHOUT ALL OF AFRICA, OPEN LAND ROVERS WERE taking astounded tourists to view the wonder of nature at its purest. Rangers from neighboring game farms were sharing their sightings over walkie-talkies.

Shut off from the pressures and problems of their day-to-day lives, these foreigners were allowed to be quiet. To look inward. To see the world in a way they'd never experienced. To commune with nature, God, and their own inner voices.

Others from around the world would get to see it through Vince Castle's lens as a backdrop for his models. Scarlett. Nikki. Brigitta. And now Charley.

Charley understood the importance of this assignment going well. And it was not only that the client was spending a fortune. She had also come to realize the importance of showcasing South Africa. As Charley had flown over their locations on the plane, she had seen a country of mind-boggling contrasts. Beautiful people living in supreme wealth or villagers living in poverty. Billionaires in hilltop Cape Town mansions enjoying the finest the world has to offer, while tribesmen in outlying villages lived on less than two dollars a day. Extremes isolated by distance and politics and religions that were as black and white as the zebra's stripes. Yet the people of South Africa were also constantly struggling to find common ground, and they were making progress.

The World Cup in 2010 had given the world a glimpse of the progress the country had made, jokes about the bleating vuvuzela trumpets aside. Now, by being included in this photo shoot, Charley would be one of the country's ambassadors.

As they climbed into the open Rover, she saw Brendan's silhouette approaching. Her heart leapt.

She nervously started playing with her hair. *Oh, God, what is happening to me?*

"Everybody here?" the ranger asked as he emerged into the light. She saw it was not Brendan but Ben, the ranger they had had when they arrived.

"Where's Brendan?" Scarlett said, smiling through her perfect veneers. "He was a lot cuter than you."

"Had to see his girl," Ben answered. "She just got back from holiday. It is amazing to see them together. Wish I had someone to love that much." Then he changed the subject. "Let's go."

The tracker climbed into his seat at the front of the Rover and they took off.

Charley had been aching to see Brendan and feel the warmth of his lips again. But he had to see "his girl," she thought to herself as her heart now sank.

The ride through the natural, rough terrain with its hills, valleys, stones, and fallen branches, was difficult as always, but Charley's mind was a million miles away.

She wasn't one to give her heart easily and, with her commitment to abstinence, had never given her body to anyone. Until Brendan, she had never wanted to. Because when she looked into his eyes, what reflected back was pure love. At least she had thought so.

He's committed to someone else? she said to herself. What was I thinking?

Charley gazed out into the vastness, her chestnut hair blowing softly in the wind. Vince's eyes were on her, and he was mesmerized.

"Stop," he told Ben as he put his hand on the ranger's shoulder. Ben didn't know why, but he did as he was asked.

Vince positioned his camera.

Charley was so lost in thought that she didn't notice as Vince began snapping photos of her, focusing on her face with its enigmatic, haunting expression. Vince saw it could be interpreted a thousand different ways, and it was perfect. The light from the headlights and the stars lit her in a way that was magic.

"That's our money shot!" Vince said with an enthusiasm he hadn't felt since he'd shot Scarlett's first cover.

"What?" Charley said as she was brought back to reality.

Vince blew Charley a kiss, gave her a thumbs-up, and then signaled for Ben to continue the ride.

From her position behind Vince, Scarlett saw and heard it all. And she knew, as clear as the African sky, that Charley, not she, would be on the anniversary-issue cover. And when Scarlett was relegated to the editorial pages, no one would be clamoring for her to do big-money endorsements.

Scarlett stared into the vastness the Timbavati, deep in thought as the wind tousled her hair.

There are millions to be made with rhino horn, she thought to herself. Who needs the limelight anyway? But as she noticed Vince clicking through the shots he'd just taken of Charley, her smile faded sadly.

I need it, that's who.

54   *JOHN, PATCH, AND SHANE*

"AND YE SHALL KNOW THE TRUTH, AND THE TRUTH SHALL set you free," John uttered as he gripped the telephone handset, waiting and hoping for Shane's call.

John was quoting the words he had held as his mantra ever since he'd seen the Bible verse etched into the marble entrance of the CIA.

"But this truth ain't gonna free you two," John said as he glanced at Jiao-jie and Wen's business card. "With luck, it'll bury you."

The handset finally rang and John answered.

"Was I right?" John asked, anxious for news.

"I'm looking for John Black," was the confused answer.

"Shane?" John asked.

"Donovan? No, it's Patch. And why are you expecting a call from Shane, anyway?"

Patch and Shane knew each other from their ISA days...not to mention that their wives were sisters. Still Shane, the erudite Londoner, was as different from rough-and-tumble Steve Johnson as chalk and cheese.

"Strange things going down over here, my friend, and after I hear from him, we may have to jump into action."

Patch looked to Joe, who was soundly sleeping on the sofa, and ignored John's request. "Is Kayla with you?"

"Haven't heard from her. Why?" John was thrown.

"We had a pretty bad fight, and she took off for the clinic. I left messages, but she hasn't picked up," Patch said with growing concern in his voice.

"Sorry," John answered. "And if she had called us, Marlena's in no condition to see anyone. The day really did her in."

They both heard a clicking on the phone.

"It could be Shane," John said quickly. "What equalizers do you have?"

"Guns?" Patch asked, startled. Having worked undercover at one time, Patch knew exactly what John meant. "I have a Smith & Wesson M&P. Why, what the hell's happening?"

"Hold on," John snapped as he clicked onto the other call. It was Shane.

"Those two have more aliases than a Vegas brothel," Shane told him.

John's heart began beating faster as it always had when he was on assignment.

He conferenced in Patch, and they quickly filled him in on John's suspicions and Shane's confirmation. The three spoke with a professional shorthand they had developed when all had worked in various capacities with Salem's branch of the ISA.

Suddenly, it felt like the great old times they'd had in Salem.

"The security code for the plane?" John asked.

Shane rattled off a series of numbers, and John smiled widely. If anyone could hack a computer system, it was Shane Donovan.

"Get over here with that M&P, Patch," John directed his cohort. "We need to check what they have stashed."

"As soon as I connect with Kayla, I'll be there," Patch said with urgency. "My wife's my top priority."

"We understand," John said as he looked at dozing Marlena.

"Better than you can imagine," Shane said, as there was a knock on his hotel room door. His estranged wife had arrived.

"Just remember my window is less than two hours."

∞

Patch realized the enormity of what John had asked him. He also felt the pressure of an MIA wife and the son who'd just gone through the most traumatic day of his life.

It was dark as pitch out now, and he was feeling uneasy.

He knew that Kayla would be furious with him for waking Joe, but since he couldn't reach her, he had no choice.

"Get home, Sweetness," he said under his breath, and he went to retrieve the pistol he'd purchased to keep in the house for protection.

Though Kayla hated the idea of guns in the house, she knew that in South Africa, a gun was a necessity in case of emergency.

Near the entrance to the hallway to the bedrooms was a large teak bookcase with a carved fascia just above eye level. Patch gave the fascia a light tap, and it flipped open. His "Military and Police" revolver was inside. He took a box of clips from behind it, put them in the pocket of his khaki vest, and jammed the gun into the waistband of his pants. Then he went to rouse his miserably unhappy little boy.

"Sorry about this, Bud," he said warmly as he reached to awaken the sleeping toddler.

But just as he was about to touch him, Patch heard a car in the driveway.

"Thank the Lord and pass the ammunition," he said wryly as he heard the engine turn off and then footsteps.

"I am sorrier than sorry, Sweetness," he said as sincerely as he could as he opened the front door.

But it wasn't Kayla, it was Beauty.

In her hands was a handmade woven basket. She presented it to Patch as a peace offering.

"Mr. Patch, I am sorry for today," Beauty said in her click-tongued Xhosa accent. "I have made this for Joe and Ms. Kayla. Please tell them I ask forgiveness."

Patch looked out into the driveway. There was a twenty-year-old Suzuki idling, with a young man behind the wheel.

"Who brought you?" he asked.

"My cousin," she answered. "He knew how upset I was and—"

"And can he leave you with Joe until we get back?" Patch asked.

"So Ms. Kayla forgives me?" Beauty asked wide-eyed.

"She will," he answered, determined to believe it. "Right now I need your help."

And I'm the one who's going to need forgiveness if she gets back here before I do, Steve thought grimly as he ushered Beauty inside.

55  *CORNELIUS*

THE HUES OF THE SKINS AND COATS OF THE ANIMALS IN THE wild have been divinely created for their protection. The white and black rhino are no exception. Large, lumbering animals who often travel in twos as they forage for the plants that sustain them, they are both closer in color to the grays of the dust that often swirls around them. Even at their size, they can hide easily during the daylight and they are nearly impossible to spot at night.

But Cornelius' tracker, Maalik, lived up to the meaning of his name: experienced. With forty years in the veld, he knew the sounds of each animal's footsteps, their habits, and the sound their silences made when they hid. He was a family man with seven children, his ailing mother, and two siblings all living in a nearby village. All counted on him for support, and this was one way he could provide for them. It was no different than hunting to him. Except that it was illegal.

Cornelius sat with Bill's Browning A-Bolt on his lap, waiting for Maalik to return.

Maalik had gone into the brush where he sat silently. Then he stealthily made his way back to Cornelius' pickup.

"Very big," Maalik nodded, indicating the size of their prey.

"And it goes to the Xings," Cornelius answered.

I'm a man of my word, he thought. Too bad that word is "bastard."

Within five minutes, the rhino was dead.

Maalik retrieved his hatchet from Cornelius' pickup and, with the efficiency of a hacksaw, had the treasured horn severed quickly.

Black rhino, he said to himself. Endangered. Maybe they wouldn't be if they weren't so big and stupid.

Cornelius stared at the trophy that would soon find its way to Vietnam or China.

This'll make them happy, he thought. And then, it'll all be for Scarlett and me.

56  *CHARLEY*

VINCE WAS ELATED WITH THE GAME RIDE FOR JUST THOSE shots with Charley. He didn't realize or care that in capturing that moment he had invaded her soul and heartbreak.

It had been a year of loss for her, and this trip was supposed to be a new beginning. Now she was feeling more isolated and lonely than ever.

They had seen the most magnificent sites in the last twenty-four hours, but when the Rovers made their way through a clearing and up a small hill for their last location shoot, what they saw took their collective breaths away. Everyone's but Charley's. That had been stolen when she realized Brendan wasn't free to love her.

The Bedouin tent was surrounded with dozens of flickering Moroccan lanterns. Inside, tables were set with the finest china, silver, and linens. This feast would include the last setups at Londolani, and then they'd all be free to party.

Several of the Xhosa staff members played stringed musical instruments, and all were dressed in white. Except for the ranger, who was chatting with the crisply dressed bartender.

Then the flickering lights cast a glow on the ranger's beaming face, and Charley could see that it was Brendan.

She felt as if her stomach had fallen all the way to her toes. He obviously had seen "his girl," she thought. No wonder he's smiling.

The models, assistants, and production crew exited the Rovers and were greeted with pear and champagne cocktails. All were happily toasting one another. Except for Charley. She was still firmly planted in the Rover.

Why couldn't I be in freezing London...

From her vantage point, she observed Brendan in all his glory. Floppy hair and cleft chin. Eyes that smiled when he did. A body that melded with her own. A body...turning toward her.

Charley froze in place. She wanted to die. She'd never been a shrinking violet, but she'd also never been a fool.

Now, there he was, smiling as though he was thrilled to see her, champagne glass in hand and walking in her direction.

Suck it up, Charley, she thought as he approached. Be nice, be pleasant. After all, he's only a guy.

Putting on her bravest face, Charley got out of the Rover to meet him.

"I thought for a minute you weren't here," he said as his eyes met hers, the firelight making him look all the more angelic. "About earlier..." he added as he handed her the crystal flute.

"Yes, about that," she interrupted. "How dare you!" And before she could control herself, she felt her hand fling the champagne in his direction.

Brendan stood shocked, doused with champagne as Charley

stormed off to join the others. "What the hell—?" he asked as he watched her go.

The scene had not been lost on the group. The girl they thought unflappable had totally lost her cool.

"Excuse me," she snarled. Her heart was racing and she was fighting tears of anger as she made her way to the bar.

"He's coming this way," Greg warned her as she reached for a fresh glass of champagne.

"Do not give that to her," Brendan ordered the waiter, who pulled back his tray. Then Brendan took her by the shoulder and turned her to face him. "And what the hell is wrong with you?"

The atmosphere was intense, and everyone froze around them. This was much too good to miss. "Do not touch me again," Charley said, pulling away.

"What happened to the girl who *loved* my touch a few hours ago?" he snapped, totally confused.

"You mean me or the girl you left me to see?" she flared.

"Phoebe?" Brendan answered. "Phoebe's my daughter, so obviously I was referring to you!"

"Well, I'm thrilled for her!" Charley was on a roll and barely listening. "Thrilled for both of you!"

"Fine."

"Fine!" she said, her voice rising.

"Fine!" he bristled.

"Did you say 'daughter'?" Nikki interrupted. "Charley…"

"Yes!" he shouted. "I said 'daughter'!" Then he raised his right hand to Charley. "Phoebe's the only girl I've been with since I was with you."

Charley was dumbstruck. The only sounds around them were the sounds of the night.

"And she's your daughter?" Charley said weakly. "Daughter…?" Her eyes widened.

"You're repeating yourself," Scarlett threw in sarcastically.

"Yes, I have a two-year-old," Brendan confirmed. "She just got back today from holiday with my in-laws, and I was aching to see her."

"In-laws?" Scarlett said, raising her eyebrows and sharing a look with Nikki who quickly shushed her.

"She's a two-year-old," Charley repeated, not even paying attention to those around her. She was beginning to feel sick for her accusations. Of course, his little girl should be his number-one priority.

"There's no stronger bond than that of a parent and child," he said matter-of-factly.

Charley drank that in. Whatever her parents were, they had been devoted to her. And she saw in the family album how much John and Marlena were devoted to all of their children.

"Phoebe'll actually be two next month," Brendan said, interrupting her thoughts. "She was barely six months old when we lost her mother."

Charley bit her lip and then turned away, horrified at how she'd reacted. "And you don't have a girlfriend…"

"What? No. The way I kissed you?" Brendan said, turning her back to look at him. "What kind of a guy do you think I am?" The hurt in his voice crushed her.

"I didn't always have the best role model in men," she

admitted. "It's no excuse, but then I'd—just seen John Black kissing Scarlett..."

"You saw that?" Scarlett grimaced. "Honey, I kissed him," she admitted. "And got nothing out of it but a blistering lecture."

Charley let that sink in. *John wasn't coming on to another woman?*

"And then Vince—" her voice trailed off.

"You and I had a misunderstanding, that's all," Vince said, cutting her off pointedly. Then he addressed the others: "Come on, we have better things to do than eavesdrop. Let's get set up for our first shots—and give these two some room."

After Vince moved away and the others followed, Charley and Brendan were finally alone.

"Who would have thought Vince could be a romantic," Charley said with a soft smile.

"And who would have thought you could be so wrong about me," Brendan said gently.

"I'm so sorry I misunderstood. And I'm sure your little girl is as special as you are," Charley offered.

"And then there's us," he said, taking her hands in his. "You and I connected in a way I've truly never felt before. Ever," he said pointedly. "At least I thought so."

Charley's knees were weak as her eyes met his. The connection was still there, the atmosphere more electrically charged than ever. It was as if every one of the creatures in Africa was now listening. A light wind swirled around them, the flickering from the candles casting a warm, romantic glow.

"Can you forgive me?" Charley asked as tears started to well.

Brendan stared at her for what seemed like an eternity.

"I should have told you about Phoebe before," Brendan said apologetically. "I just didn't realize how much you'd matter."

Brendan wiped the tear from the corner of Charley's eye, and she flicked a drop of champagne from his damp hair.

"Can I touch you now?" he asked with a smile that melted her heart.

She nodded, breathless, and he cupped her face in his hands. Both of them shuddered at the touch, and he leaned in to kiss her. It was a tender kiss that overcame them with passion.

57 KAYLA AND PATCH

THE CLOCK WAS TICKING, AND PATCH WAS NOT HAPPY. HE drove up to the clinic and saw Kayla's Jeep in the driveway and the lights inside still on. No other cars were in sight.

"You're here alone after dark?" Patch muttered. "We had a pact that you'd never do that." Then he took a deep, calming breath. This was no time for him to be angry.

He climbed out of his 4x4, aware of the chirping of nature that surrounded him. Small animals scurried across the gravel as he made his way to the door.

He reached for the door handle but then opted to knock.

"Sweetness, it's just me," he called out. "Don't worry. Joe's got someone with him," he added as a preemptive measure.

When there was no answer, he tried to contain his concern. "Come on, Sweetness, we've got to get past this," he said. "Let me in."

When there was still no answer, Patch tried the door. He was startled to find it unlocked. He pushed it open.

He saw Kayla's body on the floor the minute he entered.

"Dammit," he snapped as he flew to her side. "Anybody?" he shouted out in hopes that someone might be there. "Cornelius?"

Kayla wasn't moving. Patch put his head to her chest to make sure she was breathing. Her breathing was deep and slow, but she was unresponsive to his touch.

"How long have you been here?" he asked, with no expectation of an answer.

As he pushed back the hair from her forehead to make sure she wasn't bleeding, she began to stir.

"Sweetness, don't move," he ordered.

He surveyed the room quickly, and it seemed obvious what had happened.

"You fell over that bag and hit your head, I think."

"Wha—?" she mumbled.

Though deeply concerned, he was gentle. "Can you tell me your name?"

"Kayla Brady…" she slurred as she opened her eyes slowly. "Hi," she said with a disoriented smile. "Where am I?"

"Tom-Ali," Patch told her. He was trying to be calm, but inside his stomach was churning.

"I don't know…What time is it, and where's Joe?" she asked as she sat up slowly. Then her motherly instincts kicked in. "How is his wrist?" and then repeated, "Where is he?"

"I found someone to watch him. He's resting, and he's fine," Patch said, not telling her about Beauty.

She touched the back of her head and winced. Just then the door was shoved open. Patch and Kayla looked up to see Bill Horton.

"Kayla, are you all right?" Bill was immediately concerned when he saw her.

"I...fell," Kayla said simply. "Anyway, that's what Steve tells me."

"Make sure you get up slowly," Bill said in a calm, professional manner.

As Patch guided her up with his hand on her back, Bill extended his hand to help her stand. She was wobbly.

"I don't see any contusions, but let me check you over," he said.

"I'm fine," Kayla assured him. But she tightened the grip on his hand as a wave of nausea hit her. "I think I'm going to throw up."

Bill quickly guided Kayla to the rear of the clinic and she stumbled into the bathroom, closing the door behind her. From inside they heard her wretch.

"Lucky I saw your cars," Bill said. "I was on my way home from Ambri."

"Drinking?" Patch said caustically.

"Just two beers, same as yesterday. I'm sober as a judge, Patch." He extended his hand, which was steady as a rock. "I'm concerned about Kayla, though. The dizziness and nausea? Could be a concussion."

"If she hit her head on the floor, would there be pain on the back of her skull?" Patch asked. "Would the pain radiate?"

"From a simple fall it shouldn't. Why?" Bill asked.

Another wretch from the bathroom.

"There's a bump on the *back* of her head."

Bill drank it in. "Let me check her over. Whatever happened, we can't be too careful."

"Thank you." Patch's hand went to his vest pocket. "While you do that, I've gotta make a call."

While Bill went to examine Kayla, Patch gave John the update and he agreed that something smelled worse than three-day-old fish. Marlena had come back from the day appearing drunk as a skunk, and now Kayla was even worse.

"Not to mention what's been going on with Bill," Patch realized.

"They all have the same symptoms for no apparent reason," John said, trying to piece it all together.

"But obviously there is one," Patch said. "And it all seems to stem from this clinic."

"There's a connection to the Xings," John said, his instincts clicking in. "I don't know what it is yet, but all this happening now is too much of a coincidence."

Patch knew John well enough to know he was on a mission. And when John Black was on a mission, nothing could stop him.

"I know you, man, and be careful," Patch cautioned.

"Don't worry about me," John offered, energized. "I'm a big boy. I can handle this myself. But if you don't hear back from me in an hour…have Shane send their guys in."

Patch agreed and then hung up and quickly began analyzing the scene for clues. His mission was finding out what happened to Kayla.

He knew his wife well, and she was never clumsy. She was also a neat freak, and a medical kit would never be left in the pathway.

Bill emerged from the exam room quickly, as confused as ever.

"What'd you find?" Patch asked, deeply concerned.

"Disorientation, redness of her eyes, nausea, low heart rate— and a fresh mark on her arm."

"Mark?" Patch interrupted.

"From an injection."

It took Patch less than five minutes to find the syringe in the trash, and Bill quickly checked the medicine cabinet for clues. The meds were alphabetized and a bottle was missing.

"Rohypnol," Bill realized.

"Roofies," Patch said, as it hit them both.

"Causes memory loss and amnesia," Bill said, reeling.

"Your symptoms lately," Patch said, putting two and two together. "And Marlena's." Patch scanned the area quickly, and his eyes went to the glass on the high shelf. "Why is that one by itself?"

"The last one in a set from my parents. Brings back memories," Bill said ironically. "It's the glass I always use."

Patch grabbed the crystal tumbler with the worn gold "H" and, in the bottom, found a fine white powder.

"Bingo. He's been drugging you, man," Patch said, seething. "To keep you off balance."

Bill was stunned. "Why would he want to do that?"

"Trying to set you up for something," Patch surmised.

"With small doses," Bill said. "But to inject it…" Then he caught himself. "Wait a minute, we're in luck," he said as reached for a small vial and a fresh syringe from the cabinet.

"More drugs?" Patch asked.

"Anexate," Bill said as he headed to the rear of the clinic. "The antidote for Rohypnol."

∞

The Anexate took effect in less than two minutes, and Kayla's speech was nearly normal when she realized Bill had just given her a shot.

"Bill, Steve…" she said as she quickly came to. Her hand went to the arm Bill had just injected. "Oh, my god," she said.

"You're okay?" Patch asked, gasping in relief.

She nodded quickly, her face registering shock. "Cornelius…?" she uttered as the memories came flooding back.

"What happened, Sweetness? Do you remember?"

The anti-benzodiazepine Bill had just administered was having the precise effect that it had been created for, and Kayla began to remember everything.

Cornelius with the drugs.

Those gloves.

And Bill's gun.

58  *JOHN*

THE PAST SUMMER, JOHN HAD PUT HIMSELF THROUGH THE
grueling physical and mental tests at ISA headquarters in London to
prove to himself and Marlena that his rehabilitation was complete.
With a history that had included everything from police officer to
mercenary to art thief, this was a man who could indeed handle on
his own what life threw at him.

Confiding in anyone he didn't know intimately was neither
his style, nor smart, especially when he had no idea who else was
involved. So he opted to do what any red-blooded American or ex-
mercenary would do. He hot-wired one of the Londolani Rovers.

After the five-minute trip through the rocky Timbavati terrain
from the main camp to the airfield, he reached the jet that sat on
the edge of the runway.

Sprinting to the jet, he used the emergency security code Shane
had given him to open the outside luggage compartment. A quick
scan with a high-powered flashlight found nothing, so he quickly
disabled the steps and bounded into the main cabin.

The closed aircraft was sweltering.

Though the cockpit was exactly the same as the one he'd owned, every interior was different. Using his high-powered flashlight, John scoured the custom interior. Toward the rear, just past the rich leather sofa that lined one side of the cabin, was a wide series of shallow drawers. Using the same security code, John disabled the digital lock and slid the drawers open one by one.

Each tray held a dazzling display of gold, silver, and diamond pieces. They were works of art—signs of nature, signs of the zodiac. And one tray was filled with China's most spiritual creatures: a turtle, a dragon, a tiger, and a phoenix.

John lingered on the phoenix, a symbolic link to his past. The past, he reminded himself. No longer a phoenix to rise but an eagle to soar.

Like a computer, his mind was processing what he was seeing: symbology, mythology.

He slid open the bottom tray, wondering what he'd find. There, on its own, was a gleaming gold dagger in the shape of a snake.

Snakes symbolize a message from the underworld, John realized. Under, he repeated to himself.

He slid the drawer all the way out of its tracks and noticed a notch at the top of the steel base it rested on.

Trained by the ISA to recognize hidden compartments, John placed his finger in the notch and slid the plate open.

"Bingo," he muttered.

Underneath, he saw a large, lined storage container.

Inside? There were half a dozen severed rhino horns, worth several million dollars on the black market. Taking out his digital camera, John quickly snapped image after image of the evidence.

A quick flash of light coming toward the plane from outside caught John's attention. A car was approaching from across the veld.

He quickly reinserted the lid and then the drawer. He dashed to the stairs, pulling them closed.

He was trapped inside the jet. Without a weapon.

∞

Jiao-jie and Wen's visits to the neighboring game farms had gone beautifully. While they had sold less than ten thousand dollars worth of their incredibly expensive jewelry, they'd publicly validated their "official" reason for being in the Timbavati.

"That Meerlust at Ngala was beautiful," Jiao-jie said flirtatiously and a bit tipsy. "Can we take a side trip to Stellenbosch?" she asked as they drove their rented Mercedes back to Londolani. The glorious location outside of Cape Town yielded some of the finest wines in the world, and she'd come to love its charm as well as its vintages.

"They can send us a few cases to Hong Kong," Wen answered. "We need to get home. Thousands are waiting to pay us through the noses for those horns."

"Life is good," Jiao-jie laughed.

"No, life is perfect," Wen answered with a smile at his elegant wife as they pulled into the airstrip.

They did not notice the Londolani Rover sitting in the bush less than thirty yards away.

"Be quick," Jiao-jie said seductively as she handed him a small jewelry case. "I'd like to get back to the suite and celebrate."

Wen quickly kissed his wife and then headed to the jet. He

punched in the security code and when the stairs opened, Wen bounded up them two at a time.

Jiao-jie saw the lights go on and Wen head to the locked jewelry cases. Then she waited. And waited.

Several minutes went by, and she became antsy.

"I need to go to the bathroom," she muttered.

Making sure no creatures were lurking in the African terrain, she exited the Mercedes and headed up the jet staircase.

There, at the back of the plane, was Wen with the snake dagger held to his carotid artery by John Black.

Jiao-jie began to inch her way to the open door.

John's eyes were flashing as angrily as the diamonds in the dagger. "One more inch toward that door, and Wen's a dead man."

Jiao-jie froze in her tracks.

"Now just one little favor," John directed, cocking his eyebrow. "We're going to need the two-way radio."

Jiao-jie was not rattled. This was a woman who'd stood on the edge of danger for years. Instead, she smiled.

"We can make you a fortune," she said seductively.

"You forget," John said, laughing at her offer. "I already have one."

He yanked Wen tighter, cutting off the man's windpipe. The pain was evident in Wen's eyes as John snarled, "I suggest you hurry."

Wen's eyes were filled with panic, and Jiao-jie knew John would have no qualms about killing him.

"Let him breathe," Jiao-jie conceded, putting her hands up as she backed to the radio.

John lessened his grip but kept the dagger to Wen's neck as

Jiao-jie slithered to the two-way radio. But as she turned, she reached down and lifted a pistol from next to the seat, whirling and aiming it directly at her husband and his captor.

"Guns beat daggers, no?" she laughed. "Let him go!"

"Depends on whose holding 'em," John said as he flung the steely weapon at Jiao-jie with perfect aim. Startled, she fired, the shot going wild and hitting Wen as John released him. Then the gun flew from her hand as the razor-sharp point sliced into her right shoulder.

"Wen," she screamed as she stumbled toward the open stairway in a desperate attempt to escape.

But there, standing at the bottom of the stairs, was Patch with his Smith & Wesson aimed right at her.

John appeared in the open doorway behind her.

"Wen's dead," John said evenly. "But this one's going to need some medical attention."

"Kayla and Bill are off for the rest of the night," Patch said wryly. "But when the ISA helicopter gets here, they can medevac her."

John looked into the distance to see a helicopter heading toward them. What neither of them saw was Cornelius in his truck, observing everything from a distance.

59  *MARLENA*

MARLENA STOOD UNDER THE COOLING WATER IN THE GLASS-enclosed shower, trying to shake off her drowsiness. John would surely be back soon and she wanted to be able to love him fully.

With no one but several giraffes munching on the highest leaves outside the suite watching her, Marlena finished her shower and then dried off with one of the luxurious towels on the chaise nearby.

The sounds of the night were like music as the beautiful blonde reached for a negligee from the bureau drawer. But her footing was still unsure. She wobbled a bit, stabilizing herself on the smooth wood surface.

"Air, I need air," she said aloud, but then corrected that. "I don't need air. I need to get my blood moving."

Using the phone on the night table, she called for an escort. "I'd appreciate someone walking me to the lapa," she said yawning. "I'll be ready in ten minutes."

Marlena pulled on a simple off-the-shoulder tunic and ran her fingers through her hair. Glancing in the mirror, she slid on a pale lip gloss and smiled. She was natural and radiant.

As she slipped into her shoes, Marlena heard footsteps on the elevated path outside. The escort was a few minutes early, but she was ready so she headed for the door.

But when she opened the door, it wasn't her escort. It was Cornelius, with a pistol trained right between her eyes.

Marlena opened her mouth to scream, but Cornelius snapped, "Don't you dare."

"What's this all about, Cornelius? Where's John?" she asked.

The phone rang, startling them both. Marlena's head snapped as she turned toward it. "That could be him."

"Nope," Cornelius offered. "He's with the Xings. And you're coming with me."

Marlena gasped as Cornelius wrenched her outside with his free hand. He was adrenalized and strong, not to mention hopped up on Adderall. He shoved her down the illuminated pathway.

Under the canopy of overhanging trees, Marlena stumbled as her captor pushed her forward.

"Just tell me what's going on…"

"I was being the good guy, the honorable guy, bringing them one last horn," he snarled. "But your husband had to stick his nose in. I saw him on that plane."

Indeed, Cornelius had arrived to deliver his trophy and witnessed the Xings' capture.

"And I'm your insurance," Marlena realized.

"Beautiful and smart. Your husband's a lucky man."

Cornelius' truck was parked outside the main entrance, and he yanked her upright as they approached.

"Marlena?"

Cornelius snapped his head to see a stunned Charley in the open doorway of the lapa, Brendan at her side. The photo shoot in the tent had ended, and after their lavish supper, the crew gathered in the lapa to celebrate.

"I just tried to call you," Charley stammered. Charley's heart had been opened, and Brendan had convinced her that she should connect with John and Marlena before it was too late.

Now, the scene in front of Charley was a surreal reminder of the all-too-recent loss of her parents.

"Get back inside," Cornelius demanded as he yanked Marlena roughly.

"No!" Charley gasped as a wave of panic swept over her. Suddenly Charley bolted to save Marlena.

But Brendan grabbed her and shoved her to safety. Before Cornelius knew what had hit him, Brendan had pulled his sidearm and fired.

Bam!

And again.

Bam! The sound reverberated through the camp.

Cornelius reeled as he was hit in the chest, a wild shot from his pistol firing as the gun flew out of his hand and into the air. As Marlena was released from his grasp, he fell to the gravel, blood gushing from the gape in his chest.

Marlena's first instinct was to help her captor, but it was too late. Brendan's shots had hit him square in the chest. In an instant Cornelius was gone.

The still of the night had been shattered. Now all that could be heard were the sounds of nature and a helicopter in the distance.

Staff and security appeared, reacting to the shots and chaos. They ordered everyone to stay inside, but Charley rushed down the stairs to Marlena's side.

"Are you all right?" she said, gulping in air as though she couldn't breathe.

Marlena nodded, deeply shaken.

"Yes, yes…I'm fine…"

Flooded with emotion, Charley started to sob. "I could have lost you, Marlena. You could have died, too."

Their eyes locked.

"But I'm here…" Marlena assured her as Charley went into Marlena's enveloping arms.

At that moment, they found a new connection that could never be broken. "Looks like we both love heroes."

"I'm sorry this took so long," Charley wept as she held Marlena tightly.

"That was before," Marlena said to her daughter. "Now we can work on our new life together."

Charley glanced over at Brendan, who was now with the head of security. As he was describing what transpired, he turned and caught her gaze, and they shared a smile of understanding.

Brendan watched as the two women cradled each other, their barriers finally broken.

60 *THREE MONTHS LATER*

THERE HAD BEEN AN ABUNDANCE OF PUBLICITY ABOUT THE shoot because of all that had transpired in South Africa, and Vince's career was soaring from the buzz.

The galleys for the twentieth-anniversary edition of *The Look* came in, and Nikki, Brigitta, and Scarlett were relegated to the editorial pages while the resplendent shot of Charley was the entire cover. Vince had been right. He had captured her Mona Lisa mystique as Charley stared into the Timbavati assessing her future.

Scarlett, though, wasn't angry about the cover. Since Cornelius was gone, she'd never actually gotten involved in anything illegal. But her experience in South Africa had been a wake-up call for her, and she'd spent the past two months in rehab regaining her life and learning a new perspective.

"What do you think?" Charley asked as she looked into the camera on her computer.

Charley was in the kitchen of Maison du Noir, iChatting on her Mac with Brendan who was in the Royal Londolani library on its one and only computer. With Jackson and Chance's places being sold, John and Marlena had offered to have Charley stay at their home base in Switzerland while she decided her future.

"When it comes out, you may be a superstar," Brendan smiled as he looked at the JPEG she'd sent him.

"That's what Vince says," Charley answered. "But we'll see. You know I never wanted to be in front of the camera."

"As for me? It makes my heart beat a little faster," Brendan smiled as he put his hand to his heart and looked at the enigmatic photo. "That's my girl."

Then Charley's heart fluttered. "Speaking of your *other* girl, how is she doing?"

"I saw her yesterday, and she's doing great," Brendan answered. "That Phoebe's a little terror."

"I miss you," Charley said as she touched the screen. "How could we have connected so strongly so quickly?"

"Email, phones, and iChat," Brendan answered glibly. "We've gotten to know each other intimately without all that distracting physical stuff," he added wryly. "And believe me, those lips, those eyes, those—" he coughed "—they were all unbearably distracting."

Charley and Brendan had built the quintessential long-distance relationship. Thousands of miles had come between them, but technology allowed them to spend immeasurable time together.

"And I like who you are," she said with a smile. "Is there any chance I'm going to get to ever really see you?"

"Hey, who've you got there?" Marlena asked as she entered, flicking loose snow from her shoulders. "Is that the man of my dreams?" She smiled. "Well, he would be if I was just a teeny bit younger."

"You've got the man of your dreams, woman," John reminded her as he entered from the living room. "Hey, Brendan, how goes it there?"

John and Marlena positioned themselves behind Charley. They shared smiles, a warmth born of newfound familiarity.

"Autumn's never our best," Brendan admitted. "Thunderstorms almost every afternoon now and still the lush is turning to brush very quickly. Not the most popular time of the year."

"We've heard that from Patch and Kayla," John answered. "It's made redoing the clinic a bit of a challenge, but we know they'll get there."

Tom-Ali was finally in the midst of its repairs. Not only had John provided an interest-free loan, but when Abby and Jackson had heard of their plight, Jackson had suggested she create a tomali.com fund-raiser through *The Spectator*, and he would oversee the charity.

Although their relationship had had its rocky moments because of the Gaines scandal, money was coming into the clinic dollar by dollar, five by five, and the steady flow of cash was refilling its coffers. And even though they put their wedding plans on hold while Abby went to see her mother in Salem, the project had brought such attention to *The Spectator* and was so well run that her father offered Jackson a job at the paper.

"Everyone's really thrilled that Patch and Kayla stayed," Brendan said, giving a thumbs-up. "Tom-Ali gives a lot of people hope down here."

"Bill tells me they're planning a reopening in July," Marlena said. "Kayla's sister, Kim, and her husband are planning to be there."

Yes, Kim and Shane were indeed back together and living together in Los Angeles like the super-couple they had once been. Shane had recognized while working with John that he could still realize his passion and save his marriage by working as an ISA consultant.

"Think you'll all be able to make it down?" Brendan asked, his eyes lighting up. "Since breaking that smuggling ring, John, you're something of a celebrity down here."

"We only got one poaching syndicate. There are dozens."

"Yeah, but the international publicity you gave it helped. New tactics are going into effect on a daily basis," Brendan reminded them. "Tracking the rhinos by GPS and even injecting the horns with arsenic so that if anyone takes them, they'll be poisoned."

"If we hadn't seen all of that with our own eyes, we wouldn't have believed it," Marlena said.

"Killing animals for sport," Brendan said, choking back emotion. "Never did understand that mind-set."

"Which is one reason I love you," Charley said, then quickly covered her mouth, realizing what she had just said for the first time.

John and Marlena's eyebrows went up, and they grinned at one another.

"I love you, too," Brendan admitted. "You're my girl," he repeated. "And we can say it in front of these two."

Charley started blushing. She was obviously flustered.

"Any chance you guys'll make it back for the Tom-Ali celebration?" Brendan repeated as he fixated on Charley. "It'd be more than great to see you. To see you all."

"Four months from now, well, that's a long time in advance to plan," John said. "But if it's low season there, how about we send you a ticket to come up here to Lausanne?"

Charley's heart leapt, and Brendan was taken aback.

"I've got Phoebe," he reminded them. "I couldn't be away that long."

"I'll bet she's a good little traveler," Marlena chimed in.

"You'd send her a ticket? Really?" Brendan asked.

"Really?" Charley marveled.

"Really," John insisted. "The more the merrier."

"We have plenty of room, and we'd love to have you both," Marlena concluded as she wrapped her arm around Charley.

"You're serious," Brendan said, overwhelmed. "I'd love to."

Charley was overwhelmed as well. After the time she'd spent with John and Marlena, she'd come to love who they were and the freedom they all shared as they explored their new relationship.

"Thank you so much," Charley said, as tears of joy welled up in her cover-girl eyes.

Marlena kissed the top of Charley's head tenderly and choked back emotion. "There's nothing more important than family."

THE END

ACKNOWLEDGMENTS

Without the inspiration, patience, love, and hard work of so many people, this novel never would have happened. I want to send a huge thank you once again to Ken Corday, Greg Meng, and Corday Productions for inviting me back into the world of *Days of our Lives* and giving me total creative freedom. Lois Winslow's grace and help has been over and above. At Sourcebooks, Peter Lynch's edits and notes added clarity to the storytelling that enriched both plot and character, Diane Dannenfeldt's copy edits kept me both accurate and cogent, and ItGirl Public Relations and Klear PR worked tirelessly to promote the novel series to a broad and welcoming media and audience.

The passion with which my sister, Judy Speas, continued as my personal editor could not be appreciated enough, and Michele Reilly's input and support were more significant than ever. Lawrence Zarian's amazing friendship and contributions to story and character were remarkable, and to those who also helped with my extensive research I tip my hat. Gregory Zarian and Joe Balthazar's glimpse into the worlds of modeling and photo shoots were both enlightening and generous. Cobus Gauche, Brendan Pollecutt, and Burgert Muller's knowledge and sensitivity to both the beauty and conflict that is South Africa were unparalleled. And once again Google saved my life with facts and figures that astounded me on a daily basis.

Thanks to Paul Cohen, for his amazing humor, patience, and optimism that is infectious. I also owe a debt of gratitude to Franz Marx, who invited me to work with him twice in South Africa. They were trips that both inspired and enriched my life. To those at the Chateau Marmont who let me carve out a place to write with no interruptions in a delicious atmosphere, and to those at Roundup Valley Ranch who let me write on their porch on weekends while taking in the breathtaking Santa Ynez scenery, I cannot say enough.

As for my husband, Paca—pronounced Pay-ka—his unconditional love, inspiration, and support especially during my sporadic periods of writer's block are historic. And the glasses of wine in front of the fire while holding hands on the couch at the end of a long day remind me daily that love and romance live.

To the fans, new and old—there would be no novels or *Days of our Lives* without you.

ABOUT THE AUTHOR

Two-time Emmy-winning writer Sheri Anderson was responsible for more than 3,000 hours of network television before authoring the fiction novel series, *Salem's Secrets, Scandals, and Lies*. She is widely credited for some of the most memorable characters and groundbreaking storylines on the small screen. Shows she helmed or co-headwrote include *Days of our Lives*, *General Hospital*, *Santa Barbara*, and *Falcon Crest*. She is also a partner in CohenThomas Management, a firm representing actors in film and television. Sheri resides in Los Angeles with her husband Paca Thomas, five-time Emmy winner and owner of the media arts company pacaworks. com. He is also the on-air sidekick and producer on Bernie Taupin's *American Roots Radio*.

A Stirring from Salem is the second in the series.

*The story continues in these
new releases from
Days of our Lives Publications
and Sheri Anderson*

Available now
978-1-4022-4474-2
$14.99 U.S./$17.99 CAN/£9.99 UK

Fall 2011
978-1-4022-4480-3
$14.99 U.S./£9.99 UK

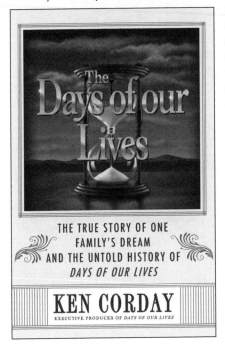

Days of our Lives 45 Years

A Celebration in Photos

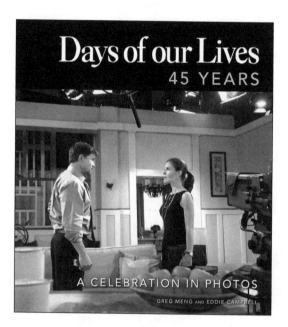

Days of our Lives 45 Years: A Celebration in Photos is an unprecedented photographic journey behind the scenes of the longest-running scripted program in NBC's history, *Days of our Lives*. Including both vintage and recent behind-the-scenes photos, this book showcases the beautiful cast, dedicated crew, and familiar sets of a television icon that continues to this day to bring the beloved world of Salem to its loyal viewers.

978-1-4022-4349-3 • $29.99 U.S./$35.99 CAN/£19.99 UK